Course of the Waterman

Course

of the
Waterman
Nancy Taylor Robson

RIVER CITY PUBLISHING

MONTGOMERY, ALABAMA

Published in the United States by River City Publishing
1719 Mulberry St.
Montgomery, AL 36106.

Designed by Lissa Monroe

First Edition—2004
Printed in the United States of America
    3 5 7 9 10 8 6 4 2

Library of Congress Cataloging-in-Publication Data:
Robson, Nancy Taylor, 1951-
    Course of the waterman / Nancy Taylor Robson.-- 1st ed.
        p. cm.
    ISBN 1-57966-052-5
    1. Chesapeake Bay Region (Md. and Va.)--Fiction. 2. Eastern Shore (Md. and Va.)--Fiction. 3. Loss (Psychology)--Fiction. 4. Fathers and sons--Fiction. 5. Male friendship--Fiction. 6. Teenage boys--Fiction. 7. Fisheries--Fiction. 8. Fishers--Fiction. I. Title.
    PS3618.O337C68 2004
    813'.54--dc22
                                                    2004009680

It's no fish ye're buying—it's men's lives.

—Sir Walter Scott

one

℃

The trotline groaned over the roller as it came up out of the blue-black Elizabeth River on Maryland's Eastern Shore. Braced against the boat's wooden coaming, seventeen-year-old Bailey Kraft was poised, dip net ready, scanning for the bait twisted every eight feet or so into the mile-long line. That was where the crab would be—if there were a crab. As he watched, a shadow rose from the dark water and came into focus, sharpening into olive shell and blue-green claws that clung to a frayed gray eel chunk tied to the line. When the crab broke the surface, Bailey leaned out, scooped it up, and dumped it into the bushel basket at his feet.

It was a nice one, he noted, large and heavy. But there hadn't been many like that. There were more empty chunks of half-chewed salt eel going *thrup thrup*, like the sound of a car passing over a distant railroad track, as they flipped over the roller on their way back into the water. Every now and then, a piece of bait was missing. Then, Bailey's father, Orrin, would throw the engine into neutral and twist another piece of bait into the line before continuing. It was their fifth pass.

Bailey liked running a trotline, even one that had as few crabs on it as this one. He loved the rhythm, the mingled smell of diesel and salt marsh, the familiarity of hard wooden coaming against his thigh. He had been on the river since he was three. Swathed in a life jacket, he toddled after his father, clinging to the bushel baskets that held crabs in summer, oysters in winter. He learned to pay out purse seines and to draw up pound nets quivering with silver-skinned rockfish and sea trout and perch. When he was six, he began driving the *Leah Jean*, named for his grandmother Kraft, just as Kraft boats had always been named for the women they left ashore. Bailey was barely tall enough to see forward. Mainly, he'd watched his father's back as Orrin stood, dip net ready to snatch one crab after another off the line. Occasionally, Orrin would stick up two fingers without looking back and point off to port or starboard. It was a silent signal of direction to Bailey and implied trust, partnership. At ten, Bailey could navigate by instinct, his DNA programmed just like the crabs that migrated to the bottom of the bay each fall.

"The boy's got the Kraft genes," he had overheard his father say.

A rare boast, it had filled Bailey with a sense of belonging.

The engine churned, slowly pushing the *Leah Jean* along the trotline. Bailey leaned out again, noting with satisfaction that he had gained about eight inches of reach since last year. His body had hardened, too, the muscles and sinews visible in outline through the skin. With a deft sweep, he scooped another crab and dumped it into the basket with the others. He hadn't lost a single crab since he was eight and had nearly fallen out of the boat trying to net one before it let go and fell back into the water. It was spring, the beginning of crabbing season. Reaching way out over the deck, he had lost his balance and slipped like a wet fish toward the cold black water. His father had simultaneously kicked the throttle into neutral and grabbed Bailey by his hip pocket just before he went over the side. Instead of yelling at his son the way Booty's dad, Tud, always did, Orrin had dragged him back aboard and merely remarked, "Nice try," before pushing the throttle back into forward and continuing down the line.

"Let's make one more pass and then take her up and go in," Orrin said to Bailey's back. "I promised your ma we'd be home for supper with the Warrens."

Boothe Warren, called Booty because of the treasures he used to find on the river when he was a little boy, was Bailey's best friend. The friendship was inherited, not chosen, the result of a lifelong family tie. Krafts and Warrens had been fishing side by side for generations. Tud had even gone out on *Leah Jean* for a while after his father died unexpectedly at forty-two. Grateful for the companionship and the chance to work alongside Orrin and Grandpa Kraft, Tud chartered out *Evelyn Louise* and culled for the Krafts for a share of the take. It was safer.

Lone fishing courts tragedy. Even on a calm day, a man can lose his balance, hit his head, and fall overboard. After he misses a meal, sometimes two, his family calls the marine police, who gathers a search party. Every waterman on the river—even if they don't like the man they're looking for—turns out, dues for membership in the community of those who follow the water. Sometimes, though rarely, they find the man alive. But more often, they find the empty boat, like an abandoned child, bobbing directionless in the water. They take the boat in tow and bring it home. Then the waiting begins—sometimes for weeks. Shackled by grief, the family silently clutchs at hope until the swollen, tattered body washes ashore.

After Grandpa Kraft died, Orrin and Tud worked side by side on *Leah Jean*. But when their sons were eight, old enough to handle the boats while their fathers worked, Tud and Booty moved back onto *Evelyn Louise*. The change had been Orrin's doing, not Tud's. Tud would have stayed. It wasn't just the companionship. He didn't have Orrin's nose for finding fish and knew it. The lack worked on him, chewing away at his confidence and sharpening his temper, a combination that gradually drove away all but a few old friends, loyal out of habit. The only one who never seemed to mind Tud's snappishness was Booty, whose determined smile rarely faltered despite his father's dark moods.

They came to the end of the trotline. Bailey netted the last crab, a jimmie—male—which meant it was a keeper, and dumped it into the half-full bushel on top of the others. The new arrival upset the calm among the others. They scrambled around, attacking each other with shimmering

9

claws, and climbing up the basket's slatted sides for a better position. After nudging one potential escapee back with his boot, Bailey covered the basket, securing the lid under the wire handles. He dropped the dip net down on deck alongside the engine box, then picked up the boat hook as his father maneuvered *Leah Jean* around the float that marked one end of the trotline. When it was within reach, Bailey hooked the float, then hand over hand brought in both float and line until he saw the cinder block weight attached to its bottom. When the block broke water, Bailey leaned out, careful not to scrape it on *Leah Jean*'s hull as he brought it aboard.

Orrin eased the helm over gently, waiting for the boat to swing her stern, letting her drift languorously into position before he put her back in gear and headed for the buoy at the other end of the trotline three hundred yards away. As they plowed slowly forward, Bailey took up the line, still baited, and coiled it into another basket.

He glanced at his father, who stood with his foot on the coaming. Orrin looked oddly gray, exhausted, his shoulders hunched like the blue heron that watched them laconically from a half-sunken stump on shore. *Tired of going out without me when I'm in school*, Bailey thought. *It won't be long before I'm out here with him full time. I can take some of the load off him.*

Once the other float and weight were aboard, Orrin prodded the engine up to full power and headed up the Elizabeth River. Bailey shoved the dip net and boat hook into the small cabin, then came back to sit on the engine box.

"Not much of a haul," he remarked, raising his voice above the clattering engine.

Leaning against the upright that supported the overhead canopy, Orrin massaged his left arm without reply, eyes on the river.

"What's the matter with your arm?" Bailey asked.

"Nothin'."

Bailey looked at his father's face, wind-etched like the sandy shores, as much a part of the landscape as the trees and fields. Though Orrin was forty-three, Bailey had always thought of him as old. Or maybe powerful—at least always stronger, bigger, smarter than Bailey. He felt as though he had spent his life trying to catch up to his father. Until the beginning of this summer. At that moment Bailey realized he had grown tall enough to look Orrin directly in the eye. It was both exhilarating and unsettling.

As they cleared Cathers Bight, Orrin cleared his throat.

"Bailey."

"Yeah?"

"I don't want you to be a waterman."

For a moment, Bailey thought he had imagined it. He stared at his father in disbelief, but Orrin, his jaw set, kept his eyes on a distant buoy.

"What?" He couldn't have heard right.

"I don't want you to be a waterman," Orrin repeated, still squinting into the distance, a muscle in his jaw working spasmodically.

The words made no sense to Bailey, like some new language.

"What do you mean?" he whispered, his voice inaudible over the rumble of the engine. He knew that other watermen, discouraged at the diminishing stocks and increasing regulations, told their sons not to become watermen, to come ashore, go into a trade, but Bailey had never imagined his father would be one of them.

"You're right," his father continued. "It's a pitiful haul. It's gonna be worse this year than last. It's comin' to an end, Son. I been thinkin' about it. I never had no choice. For a couple o' reasons. But you're smart, Bailey. You could do other things. I want you to have better'n to use up your life tryin' to make a livin' out here, blamin' yourself for what you can't change."

Bailey felt as though he had been pushed off a cliff. His head spun and he struggled for air. He was already a waterman. How could there be a choice in that? It was not just what he knew. It was what he loved.

"You've always made it," Bailey said, struggling to keep the panic from choking him. "You've got the Kraft nose. I've got it, too. You know that. You said so."

"It takes more'n a nose for finding fish," his father said stolidly, still massaging his left arm. "You can't find what ain't there. They ain't the fish or the crabs or the oysters no more. I don't want you to be a waterman," he repeated.

Bailey stared at him, gape-mouthed. His father glanced at him for a second, his expression grim.

"Shut yer mouth, Son. Yer catchin' flies," Orrin said, in an unsuccessful attempt at lightness.

Bailey clamped his mouth shut and gritted his teeth hard. Where did this come from? Orrin had been talking for years about the dwindling fishing stocks, but never in all those years had he even hinted that Bailey shouldn't make his living on *Leah Jean*.

"Take her in, Son," Orrin said, his tone flat as he moved off toward the cabin without a backward glance.

Bailey wanted him to stay, to argue, reason, explain. But he knew his father's tone. He took the tiller and guided the boat into the dock. He had tied up *Leah Jean*, left the crabs with the restaurant—two and a half bushels short of the six they had ordered—and shoved the trotline and bait bucket into the pickup by the time Orrin trudged up the dock.

"I know I ain't prepared you for this," Orrin began when he reached the truck.

"No, you ain't," Bailey snapped.

He was not defiant by nature. He had never had to be. Both of his parents had always treated him reasonably, with respect. And he loved them. But this was different. His father had cut the ground out from under his feet without warning and Bailey was flailing, scrambling to find a place to stand.

He slid in behind the wheel, grabbed the key they had left in the ignition that morning and twisted it savagely. The engine rasped to life as Orrin climbed into the passenger's seat and shut the door. Bailey pounded the gearshift into forward and stomped on the accelerator. The truck skidded on the gravel drive, fishtailing a little as he roared out of the parking lot, but his father said nothing.

two

Bailey ached to talk but couldn't form a complete sentence. Questions exploded into fragments: How could he? When? Why now? He stared at the road ahead, jaw clamped shut so hard his head hurt. He made the last turn down Fish Hatchery Road, swung into the driveway beside Tud Warren's pickup, and tromped on the brakes. Orrin trudged into the house, leaving Bailey to drag the bait bucket and trotline baskets out of the truck bed alone. Bailey heard the door slam once behind Orrin's retreating back, then again as Booty came out of the house.

"Good haul?" Booty asked amiably, grabbing a trotline basket off the tailgate and following Bailey to the shed with it.

"Nope." Bailey kept his head down.

Booty reached down into the stinking basket and grabbed the head of the baited trotline and began to feed it into a barrel of brine that sat beside a cavernous refrigerator pockmarked with rust.

"What's with you?" he asked, giving Bailey a sideways look.

"Nothin'."

Long accustomed to dodging Tud's moods, Booty fell silent, looping the bitter end of the greasy trotline to a hook on the outside of the barrel. Then he stood back to watch as Bailey fed the second line back into the salt water.

"Pop's on a tear," Booty said finally as they turned to walk toward the house. "Madder'n a hornet over the take this week. He says he's gonna quit crabbin' for sure."

"He's been sayin' that a long time."

"Yep. I figure it won't last. He'll get a good fifteen bushels and then hallelujah, it's high times again," Booty grinned.

"Dad says he don't want me to be a waterman," Bailey said, watching Booty to see the effect.

Booty stopped in his tracks, halfway between the shed and the house Bailey had lived in all his life.

"He didn't say that."

"The hell he didn't."

"Was he serious?"

"Yep." Bailey said it with conviction, but part of him hoped it wasn't true.

"Hey, Bait-ball!" Bailey's nine-year-old sister cried as she exploded out of the screen door and leaped the back steps to the grass.

"Leave me alone, Sis," Bailey said, sidestepping her.

"Get off him, Sis."

Booty grabbed her by the waist and swung her in a circle before dropping her onto the grass.

"Hey, you don't tell me what to do, Booty Warren," Sis said, grinning as she scrambled back up and charged him.

"Cut it out!" Bailey snapped, not looking at her.

"Cut it out yourself!" Sis retorted. "What's the matter with you?"

"Nothin'."

Sis studied Bailey for a moment, as she had been studying him, with envy, all her life. She'd been born with two strikes against her—second child and a girl—but she was determined, by sheer force of will, to overcome both. Meanwhile, she sought revenge on Bailey in small, strategically inflicted wounds.

"Sarah's here," she said slyly. "Mom asked her to stay to supper."

Bailey almost shuddered. Sarah. Sarah with the unflinching stare and smooth, tanned skin that smelled like new-mown hay. She was the last person Bailey wanted around. She would see right through him.

16

Just like she did when he'd shot the deer. Alone in the woods, drained of the pride-lust that had sent him there after his first and only kill, he had stood over his prey, white-faced, watching dark blood ooze onto the leaves out of the hole in the deer's abdomen. Later, he had tried to cleanse himself of his horror through the envious admiration of his classmates. He told a boasting tale of the hunt, but Sarah had only stared. Unlike the boys, she saw his pain. And shame.

He slowed his step a little, dragging his feet, trying to figure out how to approach what now had become unfamiliar territory. Did anyone else know what Orrin had said? Did his mother know? And agree? Even if she didn't, she would take his father's side. He'd never known them to argue. Orrin was five years older than Bailey's mother, and what he said was law in their house. Maybe he and Booty could take off in the truck for a while, go into town and get a soda and sit down at the foot of High Street. The screen door opened and Sarah came out.

"Hi, Bailey."

"Hey."

If he could say as few words as possible, maybe she wouldn't know he was struggling for breath, shriveling up inside.

"Bailey, what's the matter? You look all hangdog."

It was just what Bailey needed, something to sharpen his anger against.

"I don't look all hangdog," he told her, his mouth set. "I look all done in. There's a difference."

Sarah eyed him shrewdly, then looked at Booty, who had Sis in a light headlock.

"What's the matter with Bailey?" Sarah asked, as though Bailey weren't there.

"I said nothin'!" Bailey repeated sullenly.

"You can't tell me there's nothin' wrong, Bailey Kraft. I've known you since kindergarten and I can tell when there's somethin' wrong!"

"Lover's spat," Sis said with a knowing smirk.

"You get, before I take a belt to you," Bailey snapped, pretending to unbuckle the worn leather strap around his waist.

"Mom!" Sis squealed. "Bailey's gonna hit me!"

"Come on, Sis," Booty said, gently hauling her up the path. "Let's go get us some supper before you get your sassy little self in trouble."

"It's Bailey'll be in trouble," Sis was saying as Booty pulled her up the back steps and into the house.

Sarah fixed Bailey with an appraising eye.

"What's wrong, Bailey?" she urged. "You can tell me."

Sometimes, when she used that confiding, arms-out-to-hold-him voice, it made Bailey long to reach for her. But this time, it was annoying, as if she were trying to wheedle out a secret she had no right to know.

"For the last time, I said nothin'!" he shouted.

"It's not nothing," Sarah insisted.

"Well it's nothin' I want to talk about then!"

He vaulted the three steps and slipped into the house.

"Get the bait smell off in the mud room," his mother instructed.

"I know," he mumbled as Sarah went by him, head down.

By the time Bailey had scrubbed up, his mother had served his plate and poured out a big glass of milk. Not daring to look at anyone, Bailey squeezed into his place at the table. Sarah, her back as straight as a pair of ten-foot oyster tongs, sat on his left, while Tud Warren's bulk spilled out of a battered wooden chair on his right.

"Yep. Whole catch is dyin'," Tud said, energetically chewing on one side of his mouth, while talking out of the other. "We're gonna be a endangered species ourselves one of these days."

"Don't ruin everyone's appetite, Tud," Emma Kraft said as she wedged a plate of steaming corn bread onto the crowded table.

"I ain't sayin' what hadn't been said a hunnerd times before," Tud insisted. But he set the chair down on all four legs and dug into his coleslaw without another word.

"Dad said you ended up owin' the restaurant two and a half bushels," Emma said to Bailey.

"Yep."

"Maybe tomorrow."

"Yep."

"Is that all you can say?" his mother grinned.

Bailey looked up into her broad face, strong high cheekbones hidden beneath a surfeit of pink flesh, and pulled his mouth into a rueful smile. "Nope."

"Have some more coleslaw, Son. You're wastin' away to nothin'."

three

T he next morning, Bailey and his father rose and went out together as though nothing had happened. Maybe he had imagined it, Bailey thought. A Kraft not follow the water? It was just plain stupid. He had a gift for finding fish. You can't throw away a gift.

Maybe it was discouragement. Orrin didn't laugh much lately. The low catch and long hours were getting him down. Bailey had seen it before. He could wait it out. It would pass. Then it would all be the same as before. For two weeks, they went out as always—and the catch picked up. The crabs, as though in defiance of Tud's pronouncement, almost leaped into the boat from the trotline. Bailey, who had held himself taut against the fear lodged in his gut, began to ease. Nothing would change after all. His life would be on the river, an unbroken line from his great-great-grandfather right down to him, just as he had always imagined it.

Then as they were tying up Friday afternoon just before June turned into July, Orrin brought it up again.

"Your mom and me been talkin' it over," Orrin said without preamble as he shoved a bushel of fat crabs onto the dock.

Bailey stopped and involuntarily caught his breath.

"We want you to go to college."

Bailey gasped as though his father had said "We want you to go to the moon."

"Catchin' flies, Son," Orrin said to him with forced humor.

Bailey slammed his mouth shut but didn't move.

"You'd be the first Kraft with a college education," Orrin said.

"I'd be the first Kraft whose father had so little faith in him he'd shoved him off the river!" Bailey retorted, finally finding his voice.

Mortified, he bent down to grab another basket and push past Orrin to heave it onto the warped wooden boards of the dock beside the others.

"It ain't a matter of faith, Bailey," Orrin sighed. "It's reality. There ain't no life out here any more. We're watchin' it die day by day. I want better for my boy than I've had."

"What better is there than to be your own boss, to do what you're good at and what makes you happy?" Bailey demanded. He wouldn't let anyone, not even his father, separate him from the river.

"Bailey . . ." Orrin began trying to salve a wound he knew he had no power to heal. "Goin' to college don't mean you can't come back if you choose. It just means you'll have a choice. I didn't."

Bailey straightened and looked at his father.

"I love it, no two ways about it," Orrin admitted, seeing the startled expression on Bailey's face. "But I couldn't do anything else. A man should have a choice about how he pays out his life."

"I don't even like school," Bailey reminded his father.

"I didn't like school either—at your age," Orrin confessed. "But I wish I knew then what I know now. I didn't even finish high school."

"I promised I'd get my diploma," Bailey cut in.

He had already begun to count down the time until he graduated. Then he'd be free. For Bailey, the effort was a concession, a sacrifice of the time he could have spent on the water. One he had agreed to make, if grudgingly, because his parents wanted it. But college.

"A high school diploma ain't enough, Son. Not now." Orrin had a strange, plaintive note in his voice. "Dammit, Bailey, what's the good of experience if you can't help your kids with it?"

"You know, a lot of fathers are tryin' to get their sons to go into the family business," Bailey said before turning to reach for a basket.

"Not if they make buggy whips," Orrin murmured.

For a moment, Orrin watched Bailey, gauging him, but said no more. They remained silent even after they had left the crabs at the restaurant and started home. At the wheel, Bailey kept his eyes on the road, but as he turned onto the Fairlee-Still Pond Road, he darted a glance toward his father. Orrin sat rigid, his face white. Perspiration dotted his forehead.

"Dad?" Bailey asked, slowing the truck.

Orrin stared straight ahead, his mouth clamped shut.

"Dad?" Bailey asked again, pulling to a halt just short of the grassy ditch.

"I can't—," Orrin gasped, then doubled over, both hands clawing at his chest.

"Dad! Dad!" Bailey screamed, trying to grab his father as he slumped over in the seat.

"Oh God! Oh my God!" Bailey cried, his heart pounding.

He wheeled the truck around with a screech of tires, braking just before they lurched into the ditch on the other side of the road. He swore as he threw the gearshift into reverse and backed up just long enough to clear the ditch on his next try. Limp, Orrin slid down toward the floorboards.

Bailey reached for his father's shirt, dragging him back up onto the seat beside him, then jammed the gearshift back into forward and stomped down hard on the gas. The old tires screamed against the road, and Bailey was vaguely aware of the smell of burning rubber. Like a rag doll, Orrin flopped back against the seat.

With his foot pressed hard on the accelerator, Bailey turned back onto Flatland Road, gaining speed. They careered over the uneven tarmac, the bait and crab baskets jostling like frightened calves in the truck bed. Gripping the wheel in white-knuckled hands, he recited a jagged litany of prayers and curses.

They leaped the hump by the tiny radio station, barreled down the hill past the jail, then over the next rise. Bolting through the stop sign onto Route 20, the truck skidded around the turn, just missing a south-bound car. A basket flew out of the back and shattered. Barely touching the brakes, Bailey took the turn by Foster's Mill just ahead of an oncoming truck, then shot up toward the light at the main crossroads. Orrin lay in a heap, his head barely touching Bailey's leg.

"We're almost there, Dad," Bailey said, struggling to keep his voice steady, unaware that he was shouting. "You just hang on, it won't be long now."

He rocketed around the corner by the bank just as the light changed to release a long line of traffic that started moving down Washington Avenue. Horns blared, a rare occurrence in quiet Elizabethtown. A police officer who had been waiting at the light switched on his siren and sped after Bailey.

Careening down the center passing lane, dodging cars, swearing, shouting encouragement to his father and to himself, Bailey passed the Skanky Crab Tavern and the gas station, then blasted through the first stoplight at Adams College. The police car, siren howling, lights blazing, was nearly touching the truck's tailgate with its front bumper. Furious, the officer shouted into his loudspeaker at Bailey to stop. Oblivious to the siren and the officer behind him, his whole concentration riveted on saving his father, Bailey pounded on the horn as he swerved around a white-haired woman in a Buick who waited at the crosswalk light. Pedestrians and motorists alike froze to let the truck with the police car apparently hitched to its tailgate pass unharmed.

At Brown Street, Bailey yanked the wheel around, skidding up over the curb onto a manicured lawn on the corner. Tires skated on the damp grass, plowing up petunias and shrubbery and taking out a speed sign. Finally, the treads dug in, launching the truck back onto the street, where it swerved, crunching the rear fender of a parked car. Clawing at the wheel, Bailey struggled to regain control, then sped up the street, and took the corner into the hospital emergency lane at fifty, heeling the truck precariously. As they screeched around the corner, Orrin's body shifted with sickening sluggishness. Shooting up the short driveway to the hospital entrance, Bailey began to pound on the horn with his fist. At the glass double doors to the lobby, he stood on the brakes with both feet. The truck skidded to a stop on the brick sidewalk, causing the automatic doors to slid open. The police car halted just behind the truck's rear fender, siren and lights still blazing.

"Help! Somebody help me!" Bailey screamed, scrambling from the cab.

An EMT and volunteer, alerted by the truck's horn, came out of the sliding doors. Taking in the truck, the terrified Bailey, and the officer who had sprung from his car, they hesitated, but only for a second.

"It's my father!" Bailey screamed, pointing at the cab as he ran around the front of the truck.

Bailey snatched at the passenger's side door, the policeman and the EMT at his elbow.

"Help me!"

Bailey frantically tore at his father's inert body. A second EMT shoved Bailey out of the way, then helped to drag Orrin out of the truck and lay him on the sidewalk.

"What happened, son?" one asked, while the other set to work.

"I . . . I don't know. He stopped talkin' and I looked over, and he just . . . ," Bailey stammered through chattering teeth, unconsciously grabbing his own chest with both hands.

"Get an ambu bag and stretcher!" the EMT on the ground shouted toward a nurse who waited in the doorway.

After one interminable minute, Orrin was lifted up onto a gurney. An EMT climbed up to straddle him, pushing rhythmically on his chest while the nurse squeezed a plastic bag she had inserted into his mouth. Two others rushed the gurney inside. Bailey started to follow them, but the policeman stopped him.

"Let them do their work," the officer said, laying a hand, both restraining and reassuring, on Bailey's shoulder.

"He'll be okay, won't he?" Bailey asked. He was dimly aware of a strange whistling in his ears and his head felt as though it would burst.

"They know what they're doin'," the policeman said without answering the question. "We'll talk about that ride you took in a bit. Meanwhile, let's go inside and give them all the information we can."

Bailey could barely make out the policeman's words. He could still see his father's ashen face, the lips so blue they were nearly black.

"He's got to be okay," Bailey whispered, a sob rising in his throat, threatening to choke him.

The officer gently propelled him through the sliding automatic doors to the admissions desk, where he instructed Bailey to dial his home number. The buttons on the telephone seemed to be hidden behind a haze. When his mother finally answered, he could barely hear her voice. He was only dimly aware that she had screamed before slamming down the receiver. By the time she arrived, shaking and white, Bailey was sobbing uncontrollably.

four

"I should have saved him!"

Bailey and Booty sat shoulder to shoulder on the back steps. Inside, Great-Aunt Aggie washed dishes while Emma murmured thanks to the last of the mourners.

"What do you mean you should have saved him?" Booty asked. "You did everything but kill yourself tryin' to get to the hospital in time!"

"I should have saved him," Bailey insisted stubbornly.

"How could you have saved him?" Emma asked.

Bailey looked up over his shoulder at his mother, her face in gauzy soft-focus behind the veil of the screen door.

"How could you have changed any of it, Bailey?" she repeated.

"I don't know," he wailed.

Emma opened the door, came out, and sat down on the steps between the two young men. The hem of her best dress, the one she had bought for Sis's christening, floated around her thick ankles.

"You couldn't is the answer, Bailey," she said firmly. "You couldn't have saved him. The doctor told me he had a bad heart valve, that he was probably born with it. It was in God's hands. You couldn't have stopped it."

"I should have—"

"What? Driven faster? The policeman told me you were doin' seventy through town. It's a blessing you didn't kill someone."

Bailey stared at the step between his knees. Each sympathetic look he had received over the past few days had felt like a glare of reproach.

Despite his mother's absolution, guilt lay like a stone on his chest. It wasn't simply that he had failed to save his father. He was horrified and ashamed to realize that his grief was adulterated by relief. Now, he would have to work the *Leah Jean* full time just to keep the family going. He had won by default.

"I don't know."

"You couldn't have changed any of it," Emma repeated, putting her hand on Bailey's arm.

Bailey didn't believe her but let it go. Like any mother, she would try her best to make him feel okay. It didn't. She couldn't change any of it. He had failed not only his father but also his family and himself. He needed Orrin. He hadn't realized that his father's presence was protective, that Orrin was a shield against the fearfulness of life—and death. Now, Bailey was naked, his nerves exposed, his toes on the edge of an abyss that, until four days ago, he hadn't known existed.

"I won't let you down, Mom," Bailey said, looking up at her.

"You never have, Bailey."

"I mean, we'll be all right."

"Yep, we will," she nodded in agreement, her mouth pulled into a thin line.

She doesn't understand, Bailey realized. *No matter. It doesn't change anything. Now that Dad's gone, it's my job to look after her and Sis.*

Unconsciously, he was already running down the list of things he needed to do before going out the next morning—bait the line, check the floats, make sure he had enough fuel and a few tools in case the water pump started acting up again. The three of them sat in silence on the steps for a few moments. Sis came out and slid into Emma's lap without a word. The four sat in silence until the light began to fade.

"Who's hungry?' Emma asked finally.

Sis shrugged but climbed out of her mother's lap and followed her into the house where they started to rummage around in the casseroles that neighbors and family had heaped on them. Mourning food, a way to fill up the hole left by the departed. Booty got up to go.

"What are you gonna do?" he asked Bailey.

"Go out tomorrow," Bailey replied, though he knew Booty had meant the question more long-term. But one day at a time was enough for now.

"Want company?"

Bailey shook his head, afraid to trust his voice.

Booty nodded and ambled back to the pickup. He looked in the cab and sighed. Tud, reeking of beer, was stretched across the seat, snoring. Booty yanked open the door and matter-of-factly shoved his father's bulk over so he could get behind the wheel, then started the engine and drove away.

The next morning, Bailey got up before dawn and began rebaiting the trotlines. Emma said nothing. Instead, she made sandwiches and put them and a six-pack of soda into the small cooler Orrin always carried on the boat. It was odd, but Bailey half expected Orrin to come out the back door. The routine, so familiar, promised continuity. But he knew that everything had changed. As he was loading the truck, his mother leaned out the back door.

"I've called Booty," she said. "I don't want you goin' out alone."

Startled, Bailey studied her for a moment, weighing his need for solitude and some measure of control against Emma's clear determination.

"Tud'll want Booty," he said finally. "Just 'cause I ain't got a partner to crab with don't mean Tud'll give up his."

"Your daddy went out with Tud Warren for years," Emma retorted, her voice rising. "Even when he didn't want to. Tud owes him. I don't want you goin' out alone."

"I can go alone," Bailey told her.

He wanted no talk, no sympathy. Not even from Booty. Companionship wouldn't be a comfort. It would be a test of the precarious hold he had on his emotions and he couldn't face it. Not yet.

"Booty's gonna meet you at the wharf," Emma informed him, ignoring his defiant words.

"Booty can't go out with me forever," Bailey growled.

"Well, he's goin' today."

Emma let the door fall shut and went back into the kitchen, cutting off further discussion. Bailey resented her interference but realized this was one argument he had lost before it had begun. When he halted the truck beside the bulkheaded inlet at Hanson's, Bailey saw Booty aimlessly kicking stones around the restaurant parking lot.

"Feel like a baby sitter?" Bailey asked as Booty came over to help him unload the truck.

"Some," Booty admitted, despite Emma's strict instructions on the phone not to say so.

The two of them began hauling gear out to the end of the pier where *Leah Jean* was tethered.

"I don't need a partner," Bailey said, heaving a basket of trotline aboard.

"Everybody needs a partner," Booty replied, climbing aboard with a stack of empty bushel baskets, hosed out the night before to remove some of the crab stench. He tucked them into a corner of the cockpit, then leaped to the dock again to stand by the stern line. "Pop's meetin' us down at Cathers Bight."

Bailey squinted at Booty. Tud's meeting them was neighborly support, Bailey knew, but he felt that underneath it lay a need to benefit from the situation. Bailey didn't want to just give away the secrets of the river. They were too precious, the difference between making it and not.

"Tud can meet us," Bailey told him, "but he better find his own place to crab. I need room to work."

Practiced at avoiding argument, Booty just shrugged and slid the clove hitch up on the piling until the two loops of stern line opened like a magician's trick in his hands. Loosely coiling the line, he cast it into the cockpit, then walked toward the bow.

"I'm casting this boat off," he said. "If I was you, I'd fire up that engine."

Though he was annoyed at being pushed, Bailey climbed aboard and cranked it over. The engine roared to life just as Booty cast the bowline onto the deck and stepped aboard. He came down the narrow rail, balancing with careless grace, and flipped off the spring line, then coiled it up and pitched it onto the engine box beside the stern line Bailey had coiled.

Nudging the throttle up, Bailey edged *Leah Jean* away from the dock and headed down the river. The mists rose like angel wings from the unblemished water as the boat slid past Devil's Reach, then past the greedy cormorants that sat like sleek-robed bishops on the pound net stakes off Newman's Wharf. As they approached buoy 25, a small green can bobbing at the bend in the river, the osprey that had woven her nest into the top of it set up a cry of outrage. She spread her broad wings and rose to swoop threateningly over Bailey's head, screeching as they rounded close enough to see three fledglings in the thicket of feathers, twigs, and straw. The huge bird made three passes close over *Leah Jean* before returning to the massive nest that now bobbed drunkenly in the boat's wake.

"I guess she told you!" Booty grinned. "Doesn't think much of you near her babies!"

It was the first thing either had said since leaving the dock. Partly from familiarity, partly from the knowledge that they were charting new, uneasy territory in their lives, they had maintained silence.

"Dad loved a mornin' like this," Bailey said softly.

Booty saw his friend's lips move but couldn't hear the words over the engine and could only guess at the pain they expressed.

Bailey guided the boat automatically around the serpentine bends, his mind on the last trip he had taken with Orrin barely five days before. In his imagination, he could see his father clearly, bent over a basket of crabs, framed by the fragmite along the shore. He's gone, Bailey reminded himself. Yet it didn't seem possible. Standing at *Leah Jean*'s helm, the engine throbbing beneath his feet, Bailey could almost feel his father's presence. Tears churned into his throat, but he swallowed hard, narrowed his eyes, and kept them fixed on the next channel buoy.

At Spaniards Neck where the river widened, he pulled the throttle back and slowed the boat until it was drifting. Hand on the strut that supported the canopy, he closed his eyes, lifted his nose, and drank in the breeze, laden with the scents of rich, tilled earth, salt marsh, and river.

Booty watched in fascinated silence. It's like a prayer, he thought. He's waitin' for the river to tell him how to pay out his trotline. Movement in the hollow of Cathers Bight caught his eye, and Booty saw the *Evelyn Louise* making for them, pushing a lacy froth at her bow.

"Here comes Pop."

Bailey ignored him, moving forward to position the trotline baskets and scan the long reach of Rebels Neck. Tud had dropped his trotline in the bight on the north side of the river. No one else had laid out a line yet this morning. Tud pulled up about twenty feet off Bailey's starboard side and shoved his throttle into neutral.

"Might do better comin' up inside the bight," he called, by way of conversation.

"I'll be fine right here," Bailey replied, not looking up from where he worked.

Tud watched him a moment, debating whether or not to exert some kind of paternal authority over Bailey's decision, then decided against it. Instead, he made an unaccustomed attempt at banter.

"Got a new crew member there, eh?" he said.

Without responding, Bailey dropped the first float's anchoring weight overboard, then paid the trotline out gently with one hand as he walked back to throttle up and slowly run the line out parallel to the shore.

"Let me pay 'er out," Booty said, coming to take the baited line from Bailey.

"You could drop a anchor and come with me," Tud called. He had kicked the boat into gear to keep up with the *Leah Jean*.

"No, thanks," Bailey shouted in reply, his eyes on the middle distance where he planned to drop the other end of his line.

He couldn't have borne riding with Tud and especially not with Tud and Booty together, bickering, joking, caught in the net that tied father to son. Bailey wanted no reminders. He wanted to be alone with the river and his memories. He also knew that with Tud, he'd get only a crewman's share of the catch. He wanted—needed—the captain's haul.

"Well, suit yourself, Bailey. You Krafts always have," Tud said with unaccustomed mildness. "I'll be running over across the way. We can keep each other in sight."

Bailey nodded and waited while Booty readied himself beside the second trotline. Tud waved once, pushed up the throttle, and curved away back to his lines while Bailey and Booty began to pay out the second line.

At the end of the day, they came back up the river with seven full baskets. His father had been wrong. There was still a living to be made following the water. And Bailey was going to make it.

five

Booty came out with Bailey every day. There had been no spoken agreement. Booty simply came. He waited every morning in the restaurant parking lot until Bailey pulled in, then helped him heave baskets onto the boat and let the lines go. After that first day, Tud stopped offering advice or comment and just followed along in the *Evelyn Louise*, letting Bailey choose the territory, staying clear of his lines, and taking up as many crabs as he could while they were biting and Bailey was guiding his way.

They were making their limits most days, taking in more crabs than they had the year before. It was a partnership of sorts; they were making sure he stayed alive, and he was making sure they got their take of whatever crabs were there.

THE CICADAS WERE singing end-of-summer's praises when Bailey stopped the pickup in the driveway at home. His mother's station wagon was gone and in its place was Sarah's mother's station wagon. Bailey was curious, but he didn't head for the house until he had fed the baited trotlines back into the vat of brine in the shed. A stinking, messy business but economical. He could use the bait a second day. By the time he came out, he could see the outline of Sarah's oval face behind the screen door. When she caught sight of him, she ducked back into the kitchen until he had banged into the mudroom.

"Where's Mom?" Bailey asked, not looking at her as he kicked off his boots, then pulled his shirt over his head and dumped it on the floor beside the washer. Though they had grown up together, lately the mere sight of Sarah started his heart thumping uncomfortably in his chest.

She came and leaned against the door jam while Bailey, naked to the waist, bent down into the deep sink to scrub off the stench of salt eel, crab, and river.

"Your mom had to go out and she wanted me to come stay with Sis," Sarah replied, trying to sound casual.

Her heart jolted at the sight of Bailey's bare arms, at the curve of his back, the muscles working as he scrubbed himself. She wanted to put her hands on his bare skin, feel his warmth, pull him close. When Emma had phoned, asking Sarah to baby-sit, Sarah had agreed immediately. She would have done it for love of Emma alone, but she rejoiced at the chance to spend time in Bailey's house, maybe to talk—really talk—with Bailey for the first time since his father had died.

"Where'd Mom go?" Bailey asked again, still scrubbing.

He could feel Sarah's eyes on him, sense how she was standing without even looking. She had been standing the same way since she was eight or nine, her hip thrust a little forward, easy on her feet, comfortable with her own strong body.

"Don't know," she replied, grinning at Bailey when he finally looked up. "She just asked me to come is all, so I came."

"You always do what you're told?" he asked, flashing the first teasing smile she had seen on his face in weeks.

"Not always."

She tilted her head, looking out at him from the corners of her eyes.

His heart pounded so hard he was sure she could see it moving in his chest beneath the thin covering of muscle and sun-browned skin. He dried himself, then grabbed a T-shirt from the basket of clean laundry on the floor and pulled it over his head.

"Anything to eat? I'm starved," he asked, carefully sliding past her into the kitchen.

"Yeah, I made a couple of baloney sandwiches for you," she said, going to the refrigerator and taking out a plate and the glass of milk she had poured when she first heard the truck pull into the driveway.

"Where's Sis?"

"Upstairs."

"What's she doin' up there?" he asked, not really caring about the answer.

"Drawing, last time I looked. She said she wanted to be alone a little while."

Bailey frowned. Usually Sis wanted to be in the thick of things, not off in her room. Then he realized he had not heard her speak of Orrin—not once—since the funeral.

"I think she needs to think," Sarah said. "Maybe cry a little."

Bailey gave Sarah a look of such naked pain that she had to drop her eyes to the floor.

"Yeah. Maybe."

Sarah put the sandwiches and milk on the table. As Bailey sat down, his mother's battered Chevy, easily identified by the asthmatic wheeze of the air filter, pulled into the driveway. Bailey and Sarah, their eyes on the neutral surface of the table, were sitting together in silence by the time Emma came through the door. Dropping her purse onto the counter, she eyed them for a moment before sitting down in Orrin's seat at the table. Bailey felt suddenly possessive of that chair and silently wished his mother out of it, back in her own place at the table.

"How'd you do today?" Emma asked Bailey.

"Got our limit," he replied. *Dad woulda been proud*, he thought, but didn't say so.

"Tud get his, too?"

Bailey nodded, taking a bite of the baloney sandwich.

"Best thing coulda happened to Tud," Emma said, getting up to pull a glass out of the cupboard and run some water into it. "Goin' out with a Kraft again."

Both knew it wouldn't have happened if Orrin hadn't died. Emma took a long, thoughtful gulp.

"Poor ol' Tud's been just hangin' on for years. I don't know how he makes it. Course it didn't help that Lottie left him," she continued almost to herself. "It takes two just to keep goin'. . . ."

They fell silent while Emma finished her water, listening to the buzz of the insects outside.

"Blisterin' hot today," she said finally. "Air conditioning sure did feel good."

"Where you been?" Bailey wanted to know.

Emma glanced at Sarah without answering. "How's Sis?"

"Upstairs. Want me to check on her?" Sarah asked, eager to escape the prickly tension rising between mother and son.

"Yeah. Thanks."

Eyes closed, Emma dragged the glass across her forehead, savoring the coolness a moment before leaning back into Orrin's chair.

"Where you been?" Bailey asked again.

"Insurance company."

Emma took another long drink and looked out the window at the crape myrtle beside the shed. It had lost half its branches in the ice storm last winter and now stood lopsided and forlorn, still too alive to cut down but too dead to be beautiful any more.

"What for?"

"To see where we stand," Emma replied, still contemplating the crape myrtle.

"Where do we stand?"

"Not good," she answered matter-of-factly. "Daddy cashed the big life insurance policy last spring to pay off *Leah Jean*. He hated owing money. He had one policy left. It's enough to pay off the funeral people with a little left over, but not much."

"I'm makin' enough now to keep us," Bailey said, his back stiffening.

"You won't be come September when school starts," Emma told him.

"I can't go back to school," Bailey said. "I gotta work now."

As he said it, he realized for the first time that he didn't want to leave school before earning his diploma, but he didn't know if it had to do with keeping a promise to his father or with something else.

"You're finishin' school." Emma's voice was harder than Bailey had ever heard it.

"I can't go to school anymore now," Bailey said slowly, firmly, as though he explaining something to a small child. "What'll we live on?"

"You're not quittin' school," Emma repeated, tilting her head back to drain her glass. She set the glass on the table deliberately, watched the last droplets slide back down toward the bottom, then looked Bailey full in the face. "I got a job today."

six

"**A** job?" Bailey would have laughed if he hadn't been so shocked. "But you've never worked before."

"What do you call raising a family?" Emma bristled.

"I mean," Bailey began again, simultaneously trying to soothe his mother and figure out why he was so annoyed with her. "You've never worked in a . . ." He searched for the right term so she wouldn't flare up at him again. "You've always been home," he finished lamely.

"Your daddy never wanted me to work," she said. "I had a job when we were married but stopped . . ." She paused, seeming to consider her words before she finished, "when you were born."

She had never told him about the beginning of their marriage, her quitting high school her senior year, pregnant by Orrin, then twenty-three. There had been no need to tell Bailey. The baby—a boy, Orrin Jr.—died at birth. A congenital heart defect, the doctors told her. She went to work cleaning houses, a way to get out of the house and out of the grief that had enveloped her. But she stopped working when, after years of trying, she conceived Bailey.

"But I never thought you wanted to work," Bailey stammered.

Not once had he considered that his mother might have wanted to be outside the house, talk with other people, help with the bills, earn money so she would not have to ask her husband for every penny. Though Bailey knew it made no sense, he had assumed that she had been born married to his father. He had heard his father's stories about growing up on the water, stories about when he was fifteen and sixteen with Tud, and they had brought to mind a young man like himself, with the same hopes and fears. But Bailey had always envisioned Emma, even then, at home, waiting for Orrin to return. He could not imagine his mother with a life separate from the one she had now.

"Daddy always wanted me home," Emma said, softening a little. "He liked knowing I'd always be here, that he never had to come home to an empty house, especially after Lottie left Tud and Booty. Lottie's leavin' just took all the wind out of Tud's sails. I think it's what makes him so mad all the time."

Bailey had always assumed it was the water, knowing he could never be the best.

"Did Lottie work?"

Emma nodded.

"Doin' what?"

"Waitin' tables at the Two by Four."

Bailey didn't remember Booty's mother. No one ever talked of her. He only knew that one day when Booty was four, Lottie Warren had simply packed up and walked out. She had put Booty in the kitchen with the doors closed, a bag of cookies on the floor, and a note that said only "I can't do it any more I'm sorry" propped up against a bowl on the table. Neither Booty nor Tud ever even mentioned her name. Bailey had taken their silence for acceptance.

"It wasn't just Lottie," Emma sighed. "Your daddy took pride in being able to provide for his family."

Bailey knew that working wives—and their husbands—were somehow less in his father's eyes. Orrin never said it in so many words, but it was there all the same. A real man would be able to provide. A true wife would understand that what her husband provided was enough. Bailey knew he could do the same. Emma's finding a job without even bothering to consult him pricked his pride. It was as though she'd said right to his face that he wasn't capable.

"I can take care of us," Bailey insisted.

"I know you can, Son." Emma put a hand across the table but withdrew it when she saw Bailey stiffen. For a second, Bailey looked like Orrin as a young man, the pride, the quickening spirit, the determination to prevail, all written plainly in every line of his body. "But your daddy and I have a dream for you. Your daddy had . . ." She started to correct herself but her throat caught, and she swallowed before continuing. "We want you to be the first Kraft to go to college."

"But what if it's not what I want?" Bailey insisted.

Sarah and Sis appeared in the doorway.

"What're you arguin' about?" Sis demanded.

"Nothin'," Bailey replied, shoving back the chair and rising.

"That's what you always say," Sis complained.

"Leave it alone," Sarah whispered, but Sis ignored her.

"You think you're so high an' mighty, Bailey Kraft," Sis spat out. "I lost Daddy same as you! I got a right to know what's goin' on!"

"Mom's got a job!" Bailey snapped. "That's what's goin' on!"

He turned and slammed out the screen door and down the steps.

FURIOUS, BAILEY HAD bolted out of the house, jumped in the truck, and taken off toward the river. He needed the reassurance of its steady, timeless rhythms. Changes were coming far too fast onshore. He careened over the back roads to the wharf, the truck leaping and jouncing, its shocks protesting the abuse. Even with the air rushing through the open windows, the sweat trickled down his neck. His T-shirt was plastered to his back. At Hanson's he skidded to a stop. Lurching out of the truck cab, he kicked the door shut and went down the dock to where *Leah Jean* floated placidly on slack dock lines. He jumped aboard, sending a series of concentric ripples away from the hull, and went to the outboard rail to put his foot up on it, prop his chin on his fist, and stare off down the river.

He needed to retrieve the certainty of what his life was, what it should be. He didn't know where this ridiculous notion of college had come from, but Bailey wasn't having any of it. His parents—no, he corrected himself bitterly, not they—she, his mother, couldn't make him go, or if she made him go, she couldn't make him work. The thought that he could refuse to succeed at someone else's dream helped. Not much. But a little.

"What's the right thing to do, Dad?" he asked aloud, unaware that Booty, who had seen him from the restaurant window where he sat nursing a Coke and a grudge against Tud, had followed him.

"You get any better answers out of your old man than I do outta mine?" Booty asked.

Bailey spun around and nearly fell onto the engine box.

"Hey," Bailey said, staring up at his friend, who leaned against a piling on the dock. "What're you still doin' here? I thought you an' Tud'd be back to the house by now."

"Pop is," Booty said, squatting down on the dock. "I stayed a while."

He didn't want to admit that he had finally worked up the courage to ask his father to consider taking him on as a partner, a real, share-in-the-take partner. And that Tud had refused. Booty knew people felt sorry for him, the son of loud-mouthed, barely-making-it Tud Warren. He knew that Tud's friends stuck by him out of compassion. They had grown up with him, tolerated him, some liked him, but they didn't respect him.

Yet Booty loved his father. In spite of being the brunt of Tud's jokes on occasion, he understood his father's disappointment in himself—and in life. Lottie's leaving had left an ugly wound too raw and deep to heal. Booty had tried all his life to make up for their joint loss by being what neither of his parents was—accepting. Accepting of all people, of kindness, of goodness, of whatever gifts life had to offer. In all the years he had worked beside Tud, Booty had tried to please him, to help him find a little joy in life. It was his gift to his father. He had asked for nothing in return, until now. Now, the only thing Booty wanted—to be acknowledged as an equal—Tud denied.

Bailey, sunk in his own mire of self-pity, didn't see Booty's pain.

"I just had to be down here on the boat," Bailey said.

Booty shrugged. "Sometimes it helps."

"Want to go out?"

"You mean burn up fuel just like the rich folks?"

"Yeah," Bailey grinned. "Just like the rich folks. Hop aboard."

Bailey turned the engine over several times before it finally spluttered to life, while Booty let go the lines and gently pushed the bow away from the dock. Bailey eased the engine up to half throttle and tooled out into the middle of the channel just as he had seen the big powerboats that filled up the slips at the wharf do.

"So this is what it feels like to be rich," Booty said, sitting on the engine box.

Bailey looked at his friend, the torn, splotched T-shirt and ripped jeans worn soft as river moss. "Yeah."

"I like it!" Booty proclaimed.

The two laughed. For one brief moment, they felt free, free from worry about the catch, the market, the ceaseless work of living. They were just glad to be alive. Gliding down the river, the sharp, deadrise bow peeling the water open for them, they watched the ripples flow away from the boat toward shore.

"What're you gonna do come September?" Booty asked as they curved round the bend at Deep Point.

Bailey didn't answer right away. Instead he raised an eyebrow speculatively then returned his gaze to the river. His river.

"Did your dad leave you the boat?"

Bailey was embarrassed to admit he didn't actually know. He had simply assumed that the boat was his by right. But he hadn't asked what the will had said, and his mother hadn't mentioned it. That is, if his father, who had always kept those things close to his chest—like his mother, he acknowledged—even had a will.

"My mom's got a job," Bailey said, veering off toward another uncomfortable subject, but one less painful than the thought that the boat might not be his.

Booty's eyes widened. "A job? No kiddin'! Where?"

"Insurance company," Bailey said cryptically, realizing he hadn't even bothered to ask which one.

"Doin' what?"

Bailey shrugged. "What can she do? Push papers, I guess."

"What about Sis?"

Booty was unnaturally full of questions today, Bailey noted.

"I don't know. I'm not sure she's really thought it all out," he said, then felt disloyal at the criticism. "Sarah was there today when I got back."

"Sarah . . ." Booty pulled the name out on his tongue like a sweet, lingering taste, watching Bailey's reaction. "Sarah there every day when you get home. Jus' like your—"

"She'll probably be in school," Bailey cut in, unwilling to have Booty speculate about his feelings for Sarah or hers for him.

"What about you?" Booty persisted. "You gonna quit school?"

"Mom wants me to graduate," Bailey replied, though he knew it wasn't an answer. "But the boat needs keepin' up, and the bills need to be paid."

"You ever think about a partner?" Booty asked, making an effort to appear casual.

"Tud'll want a partner before too long," Bailey replied. ·

"Maybe," Booty said and looked off down the river to where the wheat fields were alight with the setting sun.

"No, I never thought about a partner," Bailey finally answered to ease the strain he could see on Booty's face.

"Well, if you ever think you want one . . ."

"You'd be the one if I did," Bailey replied.

In some ways, he and Booty had always been partners. Better than brothers since there had been no rivalry. "Cahoots," his mother always said with an indulgent grin. "You two are in cahoots again," when they started out the door together armed with dip nets that they held across the handlebars of their bikes. They were together more than apart—even before Lottie left—stuffed in life jackets, puttering around the dock while their fathers loaded or unloaded the boats.

They were together when Orrin gave Booty, then seven, his nickname. Put ashore to amuse themselves while Orrin and Tud worked, they had wandered the shallows with dip nets, dragging a bushel basket floating inside a chewed-edged life ring. Bailey, always focused on the catch, scanned the little underwater craters made by the sunfish, searching for crabs. But Booty wandered in and out of the water, sometimes running up the beach for a particularly sculpted piece of driftwood or to turn over a shell beached at high tide, sometimes reaching between his feet for a shard of colored glass worn smooth. He examined each find with the fascination of an explorer discovering a new species. Bailey was just reaching for a small peeler crab as Booty grabbed his arm and pointed farther out into deep water.

"What?" Bailey had asked, looking up only after he had snagged the crab.

Booty pointed. Something bobbed in the sun-flecked river, now glinting, now disappearing.

"What is it?" Bailey asked, not moving.

"I don't know," Booty replied, transfixed, eyes on the object. "Maybe treasure."

Before Bailey could stop him, Booty had dropped his dip net beside Bailey and dove out toward it. Bailey darted a glance toward the *Leah Jean* and *Evelyn Louise*, both running trotlines against the opposite shore. If Tud or Orrin saw Booty actually swimming—the rule was "no deeper than your belt buckle"—their shore walking would be over for a long time. But Booty had been focused on his objective. And he was a good swimmer. Bailey watched him stroke toward the floating object, grab it, and swim back, careful to kick beneath the surface so there would be no splashing. When he reached waist-high water again—just as Orrin looked up to check on the boys—he rose, holding his salvage aloft, triumphant.

"What is it?" Bailey asked, squinting against the sun.

"A bottle," Booty grinned.

Booty held it up for inspection. It was a wine bottle, corked and sealed with wax. He peered through the glass, translucent with the sun behind it.

"It's got something inside!" he crowed.

He had found some interesting things before—stones that looked like diamonds, rubies, and jade when you spit on them; bleached raccoon skulls; arrow heads; a perfectly preserved boat shoe, though it was only one and much too big for either of them. But he had never found a note in a bottle. He was delighted.

He scraped at the wax that covered the cork, but his fingernails were too soft to penetrate. Bailey pulled out his pocketknife and whittled off the wax, but the exposed cork was pushed too far inside to get a grip—or even a bite—on it. They gave up and put it into the floating bushel basket.

"Look what I found!" Booty had said to Orrin when he slid *Leah Jean* back into the shallows to collect them and their gear.

"You always come back with booty when you boys go out," Orrin observed as Bailey handed him the basket before clambering aboard.

"But look at the best thing," Booty persisted, reaching into the basket that Orrin had slid under the coaming. He held the bottle up to the sunshine to show Orrin. "There's something inside."

Orrin smiled and patted Booty's tousled head.

"Nice work, booty hunter"

When they got into the dock, Orrin had taken the bottle into the restaurant to pull the cork but returned it to Booty, contents intact. Booty took it, eyes gleaming, turned it upside down, and shook it until he could just reach an end of the paper inside with one thin finger. Carefully drawing it out, he handed it to Orrin to read.

"Whoever finds this note should contact the Horn Point Marine Biology Laboratory. There will be a reward," Orrin read. "There's an address and phone number."

"Treasure," breathed Booty.

"How big a reward, I wonder," said Tud, who had come up behind the boys.

"Whatever I get, I'll split it with you," Booty said, turning to Bailey.

For a moment Bailey had been tempted. A reward. It might be enough for that new fishing pole he had been eyeing at Dimler's store, maybe even a new tackle box, and who knew how many sodas at Shramm's. But his sense of fairness intervened.

"Naw," he said, shaking his head. "You saw it. You got it. It should be yours."

Orrin had caught his eye and winked approvingly.

"Biology lab. Not likely to be much anyway," Tud warned, unwilling to let his son's hopes fly too high.

Booty's face had dimmed at the words.

"Ya never know," Orrin said, patting Booty's shoulder. "It might not be money but it might be something really interesting. Either way, it's all yours Booty boy."

Booty had beamed, hope restored.

A partner. Bailey looked at Booty now, sitting on the engine box, face turned into the false breeze created by their forward motion. He was still determined to find the treasure in life. If he ever did want a partner—other than his dad—Booty would be it. But he hadn't thought about a partner, though Booty had been out with him every day. Accepting a partner would be accepting Orrin's death, and Bailey just wasn't ready. Instead, he had been just keeping on, baiting lines, laying them out, trying to keep things going the way he believed Orrin would have wanted. The way Orrin would have done if he were here, as though he could still return.

Talking about a partner brought the finality of Orrin's death home with sudden painful clarity, an acknowledgment that nothing would ever be the same again. He had been telling himself that he understood that, but each time it hit him, it felt like a sledgehammer right to the chest. Wordlessly, Bailey pushed on the stick and swung *Leah Jean* in a wide arc, heading her back upriver.

"Can't pretend to be rich folks for too long," he said. "Too expensive."

seven

The next morning, Bailey had reached the truck with his cooler before Emma leaned out the door.

"Wait for Sis!"

"What do you mean, 'Wait for Sis'?" Bailey asked, dragging the driver's side door open against protesting hinges.

"I'm not gonna be here most of the day," Emma told him. "She's goin' with you."

"With me? What am I gonna do with her?"

He saw his mother's eyes narrow and knew he'd gone too far—he was actually fond of Sis to a point—but was desperate to stave off what seemed like an avalanche of change.

"Teach her to crab," Emma retorted. "And if I hear you've been mean to her, Bailey Kraft, I'll have your hide."

She slammed the door and went back inside. In a few moments, Sis, clutching a small cooler, shoulders squared and chin thrust out like the figurehead on the *Mayflower*, came out the door and down the steps.

"This wasn't my idea," she grumbled, trying to keep her older brother from making her feel more unwanted than she did already.

"Just get in."

Sis went to the passenger's side door and yanked it open. She hesitated a second when her eyes fell on the empty seat where her father had died, but shooting Bailey an angry look, she pursed her lips and climbed in. They rode to the wharf in silence, broken only once by Sis's reiterated protest that her coming had not been her idea. Bailey seethed.

It wasn't enough to lose his father. Now, his mother had begun taking over his life.

For the entire fifteen-minute ride, Sis hunched in the passenger seat, pressed against the door as far from her brother as she could get. Bailey stopped at the wharf and jumped out. Wordlessly, Sis scrambled out and trotted down the dock after Bailey, still clutching her cooler in one hand and the bushel basket he had handed her in the other. She climbed aboard *Leah Jean*, dropped the basket and the cooler on the deck, and sat on the engine box, hugging her knees to her chest protectively and watching Bailey's every move. Methodically, he finished loading the gear, started up the engine, and cast off, coiling the lines while he eased the boat away from the dock with his hip pushing gently against the tiller. He wondered where Booty was and felt slightly guilty that he hadn't waited. But he was relieved that he was finally alone—sort of—on *Leah Jean*. Maybe Mom called Booty, Bailey decided, told him I wasn't going to be alone today. I've got to do something about her interfering.

"What do you want me to do?" Sis asked finally, popping open one of the sodas her mother had put into the cooler with her sandwiches.

"Nothin'," Bailey muttered.

"What?"

"I'll tell you when I need you to do something," he replied, raising his voice over the hammering engine.

Sis nodded. Lifting her face up to the soft breeze, she looked across the marshes, and for one heart-stabbing moment, Bailey could see his father's jaw, the set of his father's head in Sis. As they rounded Melton Point about six miles downriver, Bailey noticed Sis studying the buoys, saying the numbers to herself the way she did when memorizing poems or math facts for school. *She wants to learn*, he realized.

"Want to see a chart?" he asked.

"Chart?"

"Yeah. You know. Road map of the water. There's a chart book on the bunk," he said, pointing toward the cabin. "Go get it an' I'll show you where we are."

Most watermen didn't carry charts. They were superfluous. Having spent their lives crossing and recrossing the same territory in fog, sleet, snow, and darkness, they could navigate by feel. Though the Krafts could do it—and better than most—Orrin had taught Bailey to navigate by chart with compass and parallel rules, too. "Even if you can do it by feel, I want you to be able to chart your course," he had told Bailey more than once. "It's good to have a back-up. And knowing the charts helps you to keep a handle on where you are, at least approximately. Nature can blindside you if you're not careful. You gotta at least try to work out where you are and where you need to be."

When Sis came back up on deck with the tattered chart book held like the Grail between small, uplifted hands, Bailey laid the book on the engine box. He raised his arm to point at the red buoy just ahead as they curved around a jutting point of land.

"See that?" he asked as the buoy crossed their bow from starboard to port.

Sis looked up and sighted down his arm.

"That's it," he said, putting his finger down on the chart, "right there. Number twenty-four. All the nuns are even numbers."

"Why?"

"I don't know," Bailey shrugged.

"No, I mean, why's it called a nun?"

"Oh. Dad told me it's 'cause the clothes Catholic nuns used to wear made 'em shaped just like the buoys."

"Were they dressed in red?"

"I don't know," Bailey said again, annoyed at having to admit ignorance to his little sister. He wished his father were there to consult. But then, if his father had been there, Sis would have been home with his mother where she belonged. Where they both belonged.

Sis watched Bailey, hoping for more enlightenment, but he had stopped talking. They rode along in silence, Sis alternately studying Bailey's face and the still incomprehensible lines and colors and dots on the chart.

"How do you know which way to pass it?" she asked finally as the buoy slid down their port side.

"Right red returning," Bailey replied cryptically.

"What?"

"Right red returning's a short way to remember that when you're coming back into a port, or up a river, you leave the red buoys to the right side of the boat, the starboard side."

"Oh."

She looked down at the chart book spread across her lap.

"I wish Daddy'd had me out at least once," she said to the smudged page. She looked up at Bailey with an expression somewhere between resentment and disappointment. "He took you all the time. But I never got to go out with him."

"You did too! I remember he took you out one day when school had some dumb thing about taking your daughters to work."

Sis shook her head.

"I got sick and couldn't go."

"But you went another time?"

She shook her head again. Bailey looked at his sister, the wide brown eyes like dark beacons in a small, intense face. With an odd mixture of satisfaction and chagrin, Bailey realized that Sis was shut off from the biggest part of their father and of their joint Kraft heritage. Sis knew Orrin's love for the work and for the water only because of his

shoals and buoys, then hugged the north shore as the Elizabeth River broadened, passing the entrance to Peterson Harbor before finally sliding on out into the glassy calm of the Chesapeake Bay. They turned north past C3, the can marking the watery ledge that surrounded Torys Prize, the diminishing island at the bottom of the long neck that jutted into the Elizabeth River. It had been home to one of the few Tory sympathizers during the Revolutionary War. The man had been tarred and feathered, a treatment that eventually killed him, and his family had been burned out of the house that had once commanded such a magnificent view of both the river and the Chesapeake. Torys Prize, empty now, had been declared a wildlife sanctuary several years back and was visited every year by thousands of school children. As the can receded behind them, Bailey slowed *Leah Jean* to a crawl.

"What're you doin'?" Sis wanted to know. Her head had begun to ache from the engine's rattle, but she refused to admit it to Bailey.

"Gettin' set to pay out a trotline," he answered, careful to keep the irritation out of his voice. He didn't like to talk while he worked; it was a distraction and kept him from hearing the quiet music of the water against the boat's hull.

"Can I help?" Sis asked, scrambling off the warm engine box to peer into the basket of eel. "Yuck."

"If you're gonna make comments, you can get back on over there," Bailey told her, nodding toward the engine box.

"Okay! Okay! What're you doin' now?" she asked as Bailey fed the baited line back into the basket until he came to one end.

He ground his teeth, then replied through pursed lips.

"This here's the float," he said, holding the float up for her inspection. "And this here's the weight," he pointed to the cinder block at his feet. "I'm fixin' to dump 'em both over then feed the line out."

"Oh," Sis said, reaching down to heft the cinder block.

"Watch out for my feet!" Bailey cried. "Here, just stand back and watch for a bit."

"Okay," she said, head drooping like a wind-flattened reed.

Bailey paid out the trotline south to north, in his mind's eye running along the underwater ledge before the bottom shoaled up to the island. Sis watched carefully, cataloguing each part of the operation, storing each step in her well-ordered mind. They made pass after pass, with Bailey standing just ahead of the overhead support, dip net in hand, operating the boat with his hip against the tiller. After the fifth pass, Sis began to fidget.

"Let me do some, Bailey," she said, plaintively.

"Eat a sandwich," Bailey replied without looking at her. He leaned out again and scooped a crab off the line. The next piece of bait was empty, but the one after that had two crabs on it, which Bailey gently pushed off back into the water.

"What'd ya do that for?" Sis cried. "That was two!"

"Doubler," Bailey replied. "A male and female mating. Making new crabs. Don't want to interrupt." He grinned at her.

"That's disgusting!" she said, wrinkling her nose.

"That's what keeps us alive," Bailey replied. "You got to look out for the crabs and the fish or they won't be around to catch."

"It's still disgusting," Sis insisted.

The sixth run returned only a few crabs—time, Bailey decided, to move on. Putting the dip net down on the deck, he headed back for the southern float.

"What're you doin'?" Sis demanded.

"We're gonna move. Find another spot."

"Can I help?"

He started to say no, but her face, hopeful, eager, softened him.

"Yeah, okay. I'll pull up the float and the weight, and you feed the line down into the basket."

He thought she'd object, not wanting to touch the slimy bait, but instead, she positioned herself by the reeking basket and waited, trying to anticipate each step in the process. Bailey brought *Leah Jean* around. When the float came within reach, he leaned over and grabbed it where it connected to the anchor line. Propping one foot up on the narrow deck, he pulled it in, carefully keeping the cinder block from scraping *Leah Jean*'s hull as he brought it aboard. Sis watched, then gingerly took the end of the trotline from Bailey when he handed it over.

"Feed it in hand over hand clockwise," he told her, making a clockwise motion as an example. "I'll take it slow."

Sis began pulling the line, dropping it into the basket in carefully fashioned coils, her hands soon stinking from the rotting bait. As he came to the second float, he slowed the boat, ready to pull it aboard, but Sis was too quick and reached overboard to grab at the float. Bailey wasn't ready for it. In one fluid motion, she slid overboard into the dark water.

eight

"**S**is!"

He jammed the engine into neutral. Could she swim? Bailey couldn't remember. He jumped over after her. The water was opaque. Where was she? She had gone right down here, hadn't she? He clawed in the darkness, grabbing at nothing, scraping his knuckles on the barnacled bottom. Where was she? His heart pounded, using up the air he had gulped hastily before going in. *Please, Daddy, please help me find her. God, don't let her drown!*

Though his lungs screamed for air, he kept searching. His hand touched a fish—no! a piece of cloth. Snatching at it, he twisted it into his grip. It was heavy. Lungs bursting, he yanked it toward him and kicked to the surface.

Sis was limp when they broke the water, eyes closed, but then she sucked in a great breath, spluttering, and began to cough and gasp. Fear throbbing in his ears, Bailey held her above the water and kicked toward the drifting boat. Reaching up, he clutched the gunwale, hanging on and pulling Sis close. Still choking, eyes wide now, Sis spat out water and sucked in air with fierce determination, both hands dug into Bailey's shirt.

"You okay?" he demanded, fierce in his terror.

Unable to speak, Sis nodded.

"Dammit, Sis—"

He stopped. Somewhere in the back of his mind he heard his father's words: *Nice try*.

"Let go of me and hold onto the rail," he instructed brusquely.

Sucking in air, still weak, Sis nevertheless did as she was told and grasped the raised wooden edge of the boat with both hands. Reaching down, Bailey grabbed the seat of her pants and pushed her up out of the water until she was draped like wet laundry over the deck, her legs still dangling down into the shimmering river. Retching once, she pulled first one leg then the other up onto the deck, then tumbled into the cockpit where she lay on her side until Bailey had pulled himself aboard and stood over her.

"You've just filled your quota," he told her. "You get one overboard in a lifetime. That's it. At least you got yours in warm water. It's not so much fun in winter."

"It stings," she said finally, when she had gotten her breath back.

Blood oozed from a dozen barnacle gashes in her arms and legs and dripped onto the deck.

"Mom'll skin me alive if she sees you like this," Bailey said. *Maybe she'll be scared enough to keep Sis from coming again.* Four hours ago, Bailey would have rejoiced at that thought, but now he was not so sure. "Get below and pull out the first aid kit. It's down there behind the sink. And get some antiseptic on those scrapes. That stuff gets infected real easy."

He reached down and pulled Sis to her feet, glad to see the color was returning to her cheeks and she was breathing more normally. Sis daubed at her wounds while Bailey brought in the rest of the unattended trotline that had begun to feed itself out again, then hauled the second float and cinder block aboard.

"Mom'll never let me go out again if she knows," Sis said, coming back up.

You're right, he thought. *And Mom couldn't work if she had to stay home and take care of Sis. I'd have to quit school.* It seemed so logical. And so easy.

And unfair. He had not realized, until he had begun to tell Sis their story, how much continuity meant to him. He had no brothers, and it would, he hoped, be years before he had a son who could follow him out on the water. Sis deserved to know something of her own history. She deserved a shot. And, tickling at the back of his mind was the possibility of a partner, a real Kraft partner—at least until she grew up and got married. By then, maybe he'd have his own son and things would have come round the way they were meant to. By the time they were approaching the wharf in Elizabethtown, Bailey had made a decision.

"Sis, you tell Mom you fell off the back of the truck while we was loadin'," he told her. "That you got all scraped up when you fell onto the gravel. And from now on, you wear a life jacket out there, until I teach you how to swim. I can't believe you don't know how to swim!" he added in exasperation.

Bailey was an honest person. He hated to lie, had never really felt he had to until now, and it rubbed his conscience raw even as he thought about it. Wide-eyed, Sis agreed and sat meekly on the engine box while Bailey tied *Leah Jean* to the dock and began unloading their catch.

He was nervous, afraid that at any moment someone who could tell Emma a different story about Sis's wounds would come along and see Sis before they had finished loading the truck. But by the time they had shoved the last basket of bait into the truck bed and slammed the tailgate shut, he had begun to breathe a little easier.

"How in the Sam Hill did you ever get so mauled-lookin', little girl?"

It was Tud Warren, followed at some distance by Booty. They were coming across the parking lot from the direction of the restaurant. Sis shot Bailey a pleading look, stepped a little behind him, and clamped her mouth shut.

"Fell out of the truck while we was loadin'," Bailey said, uncomfortable with the lie but annoyed at Tud for being there and for noticing in the first place.

"Truck, huh?" Tud drawled skeptically, peering around Bailey at Sis.

"Yeah," Sis piped up, her face flushing as she warmed to the tale she was about to embroider. "Bailey was just flingin' stuff in the back and accidentally hit me and I lost my balance."

"Don't look like no fallin'-out-of-a-truck scrape to me," Tud said, eyeing Sis's arms and legs, striped with cuts and antiseptic. "Them's barnacles."

"They aren't," Sis cried, her defiance taking Bailey by surprise. "They're scrapes from the parking lot. Mom'll be mad at Bailey but it wasn't really his fault because I wasn't payin' attention, and I fell. So there."

"Where'd you get the stuff you decorated 'em with?" Tud asked, unconvinced.

"The boat," Sis continued. Bailey had never seen her like this. "We went back out to *Leah Jean* and got the first aid kit and took care of 'em. What's it got to do with you, anyway?" she demanded.

Tud's eye narrowed.

"Watch yer mouth, little girl," he growled, a shadow of fury crossing his brow.

"She didn't mean nothin'," Bailey said, hastily. "Shut yer mouth, Sis, and get in the truck," he said.

Sis, stiff-backed and tight-lipped, shot Bailey a look of fierce resentment at his sharpness but went down the driver's side and around the front of the truck, as far away from Tud as she could get, before pulling open the passenger's door and climbing in. During the whole exchange, Booty had stayed back and watched, saying nothing. Bailey turned without another word and went to the driver's side, got in, and started the engine. He was curious about why Booty hadn't been waiting for him earlier that day but didn't want to prolong the conversation now.

"If yer mama had any sense, she'd keep you home," Tud called after them as they roared out of the parking lot.

Bailey and Sis rode in silence until they turned off Route 20 onto Flatland Road.

"Think Tud'll tell?" Sis asked as they chugged up the hill past Mike's Auto.

Bailey glanced at her.

"He might," he said, mentally weighing the chances. "He don't like bein' talked to like you did."

"Well, I don't care!" Sis exploded. "What's it his business, anyhow?"

"It's nothin' to do with his business," Bailey explained. "He just don't like bein' talked to like that, and Mama wouldn't want you to either."

"Well, he had it comin'!" Sis retorted, angry—both at Tud and at what seemed to be Bailey's disloyalty.

"I didn't say he didn't," Bailey replied reasonably. "I just said he don't like bein' talked to like that, especially not from a little kid, and he may look for a way to get even."

"Oh."

Sis thought that over for a minute.

"Mama'll believe us and not him, won't she?"

Bailey waited a moment before replying. The truth was, he knew Emma had more faith in their honesty than in Tud's. But then again, he knew they were about to tell her a lie.

But by the time Emma got home that night, Sis had eaten a sandwich and was already collapsed in bed. Saved, Bailey thought, as he sat in the milky-thin light of the shed rebaiting the trotlines for the next day. He heard the car pull into the driveway, but it wasn't until a half-hour later that his mother appeared in the shed's narrow doorway, shoulders slumped. Bailey looked up from his work.

"What kept you so long?" he asked.

"I stayed after work, learning the setup," Emma said. "I knew you two were together, so I didn't worry. You weren't worried about me, were you?" she asked gently.

"No," Bailey lied. "But it woulda been nice if you'd called."

"You're right," she acknowledged, rubbing a hand over her face as though to wipe away the exhaustion, or maybe the years. "I would've been all down your back if you'd done that to me."

Bailey nodded without looking up. He still knew the lie he held in reserve for her and didn't want her to see it in his eyes. But he had a question in reserve, too. One that had been eating at him for two days, ever since Booty had brought it up.

"Mom?"

"Yeah, Bailey?"

"Did Dad leave me the boat?"

nine

Emma paused and took a long, deep breath.

"He didn't, did he?" Bailey whispered, seeing the answer in her face and barely able to believe the injustice of it.

"Your Daddy didn't believe in complicating things—," she began.

"How complicated would it have been to leave me the one thing that should really be mine?" Bailey cried.

"Bailey . . ."

"So, what's the deal?" he asked softly, his hands rigid, halted halfway through clove-hitching a piece of eel onto the line.

"He left everything to me so I could take care of you and Sis the best way I knew how," Emma told him.

"Including *Leah Jean*."

"Including *Leah Jean*."

Bailey turned away, bitter tears starting down his cheeks.

"Bailey—"

"No!" He flung an arm out behind him as though to push her away.

"He wanted you to have a choice, to have options," she continued calmly, relentlessly. "Education could give you that. If you went to college and then decided to come back, well, that's different. But he knew if he left you the boat, there would never be anything else."

She took a step toward him, but he heard her and stiffened. Emma looked at her nearly grown son, his back a wall of resistance. Defeated, she backed into the doorway.

"He loved you as much as his own life," she told Bailey. "He did it out of love for you."

Unable to speak, Bailey only shook his head. The lie didn't seem so bad now. He was fighting for his inheritance.

"Sis did pretty good today," he began. "Of course, she fell out of the truck when we was loadin' at the end. She got a little scraped up, but we put some stuff on it and she's fine."

"She's okay?" Emma repeated.

"Yeah." That much was true.

"Good."

Emma turned and trudged back to the house, leaving Bailey to finish baiting.

FROM THEN ON, Bailey and Sis went out together every day and Booty returned to *Evelyn Louise* and Tud. Bailey had begun to respect the way Sis watched, striving to mimic his every move. She didn't chatter, either, breaking his concentration. She stayed silent until she had a question. And when he answered, she listened and remembered. Bailey, who had been learning all his life, decided he liked being the teacher for a change. There was pleasure in knowing and in imparting that knowledge to a willing pupil.

And the crabs were good. They were getting nearly half again as much per bushel as last summer. Bailey carefully counted out the take each day and once a week deposited the money to his own account—to be used for the household, certainly, but at his discretion and direction, not at his mother's. He was tired of being told what to do. But Emma didn't ask him for anything. She bought the food and paid the bills without a word about money. He had no idea what she was making—it couldn't be much—but it must be enough. He itched for a resolution between them, a settling of who was in charge, but it just hung there, ghostlike, present but unacknowledged.

As September drew near, he began to think about oystering and how to work a daily run to the tonging beds into his schedule. He'd be able to go out before school started and then go out after school, too. No sports. He hated working in the dark, but for now, he had no choice. Maybe he'd skip a day or two of school every couple of weeks. His grades might suffer, but he was pretty sure he'd graduate anyway. He would have fulfilled his promise. They—she, he amended mentally—didn't have a right to expect anything more.

Leah Jean was sliding up the river past the brick manor at Cathers Bight when Sis turned to Bailey and asked, "After school starts, then what?"

"What do you mean, 'then what'?"

"I mean, how're we gonna go out?"

"We ain't gonna go out," Bailey said, leveling what he assumed was a paternal gaze at his nine-year-old sister. "I'm goin' out. Tongin' starts the fifteenth of September. Crabs are gonna go early this year, I think."

"You need me," Sis said.

Bailey would have laughed but restrained himself.

"I don't need you, Sister. Though," he added at the hurt and anger he saw rise up in her, "you've been a good help out here, no denyin'. You're a quick learner."

He thought the compliment would pacify her, but she was not so easily mollified—not when she had made a decision.

"I've got a lot more learnin' to do, Bailey," she told him with stunning authority. "You're startin' oysterin'. I've never been oysterin'. I need to know it all. I'm just as much Kraft as you."

You are that, Bailey acknowledged silently.

"I don't know if we could work it out, Sis," he finally told her. "I been thinkin' about how I'm gonna work and go to school, too. I've got to start out nearly as soon's I go to bed at night just to get in enough time."

"If you can do it, I can," Sis said, her jaw jutting defiantly.

Bailey looked at his sister for a few moments, admiration for her growing as he realized the conviction behind her words.

"Mom'd have my hide if I dragged you out of bed," he said gently, though his voice was loud enough to surmount the noise of the engine. "You're the one who's always been the A student. It'd kill her if your grades slipped now."

"My grades won't slip," Sis retorted.

She had always been a hard worker, eager to please, organized; but there was a defiant streak in her, arising, Bailey began to realize, from a keen sense of what was just. She was indeed as much Kraft as he was, seemed to have a feel for the boat and the water, moved as though she had been aboard for years, walking easily down the narrow deck when she cast off, paying out the trotline, coiling it back without comment. She had begun to get the motion of snatching crabs off the line with swift grace, smooth enough to keep them from spotting their end coming yet fast enough to catch them in mid-air if they tried to escape. And she loved it, drank it in like some creature long deprived of nourishment. Bailey could see it in her face when she watched the water, sparkling and pleated with waves, when she nodded unconsciously as she deposited another crab on top of their growing catch, and when she leaned back and sucked in deep, satisfying draughts of salt marsh air as they chugged upriver for home.

"If anybody's grades are gonna slip, it's yours, Bailey."

She said it practically, without irony; they both knew it was true. Bailey had always been an indifferent student. In the subjects he liked, he excelled, but they were few. Mostly, he did well enough to keep people off his back—a middle-of-the-road student who caused no trouble was also no cause for attention. Though he accepted the truth of her words, the accusation stung.

"I can keep up my grades and graduate and still fish," he told her.

"Well, so can I. Better'n you maybe. Why don't we just see?"

She had him, Bailey realized. And, though he was reluctant to admit it, he would be glad of her company.

"Mom may have something to say about it," Bailey replied, conceding the argument.

"I'll take care of Mom," Sis told him, a sly grin spreading across her face.

This I gotta see, Bailey thought, but he merely smiled and headed for home.

It was late afternoon by the time they got there. They were surprised to see Emma's car sitting in the driveway. Since she had begun working, she hadn't been home before six-thirty every evening. More surprising was Tud's pickup parked cozily beside the car, a familiarity that galled Bailey.

"What's Tud doin' here?" Bailey muttered under his breath.

They unloaded the bait and stowed their gear, then trudged up the back steps and into the mudroom.

"That you, Bailey?" Emma's voice had a strange, false lilt in it.

"Yeah," Bailey responded.

"Come on in, Son."

"I'm comin'," Bailey replied. "You don't want me in there smellin' of crabs and bait, do ya?"

Sis gave him a questioning stare, but Bailey shrugged, shook his head, and bent over the sink, leaving room for her to squeeze in beside him and scrub off the worst of the stench. There were no voices in the kitchen, just a peculiar silence that hung like a threatening storm. When they finally came through the doorway, they saw Booty sitting at the table.

"What's this?" Bailey asked.

Emma and Booty exchanged glances, and Emma cleared her throat.

"Booty and me been talkin'," Emma began. Remembering that she was sitting in Orrin's chair, she straightened and started again. "Booty wants to buy a share in the *Leah Jean*."

Bailey's throat constricted.

"What? I told you if I was ever lookin' for a partner, it'd be you," Bailey said angrily. "That was the end of it. What'd you have to go bring Mom into it for?"

"She's the one owns the boat," Booty replied. Though his look was level, his shoulders were hunched, guarded.

"Mom, there's not gonna be room for Booty," Sis said briskly, raising her voice when she could see her mother begin to object. "Bailey and me decided we're gonna keep working before and after school. If I'm with Bailey, I'll make sure he gets to school on time and we both get good grades and he graduates," Sis said in a rush of logic that Bailey would have found impressive if he weren't so appalled at his mother.

"Booty's gonna quit school and fish during the days," Emma replied. "We'll have shares of his catch, and you can finish high school, Bailey."

"I just told you," Sis cried. "We've already decided we can do this!"

"It's my decision to make, not yours, Sis," Emma replied firmly. "Booty and I've talked it over and it makes sense."

"It doesn't make sense," Bailey nearly shouted. "He's got a father. He can go shares with him, he's got a ready-made partner."

"Tud turned him down," Emma said.

Bailey's eyes widened and he halted for a second. He looked at Booty, who shrugged uncomfortably.

"Just because Tud Warren's a idiot don't mean we have to take him on—no offense, Booty," Bailey said.

Booty remained silent, eyes watching. But he was stung, and everyone in the room could see it.

"It makes sense," Emma repeated, refusing to be derailed.

"Why?" Bailey demanded. "Why does it make sense for Booty to quit school and not me? Huh? If we need the money so much, I'm the one should be quittin' and supportin' the family. Not him. *Leah Jean* was Grandpa Kraft's boat. The only partner he had was another Kraft. And that's the only partner I'm gonna have, too."

"Me," Sis prodded, elbowing Bailey.

"Yeah," Bailey agreed absently.

"It's not your decision." The look on Emma's face was a mix of agony and determination. "I own the boat. And I'm the head of this family."

Furious at the betrayal, Bailey spun on his heel and slammed out of the house. They could hear him start the truck and squeal out of the drive. Sis turned to her mother, fists on hips.

"How could you sell us out?" she demanded.

"Watch your mouth, young lady," Emma growled, her face hardening.

"Mom, how could you do this without even talking it over with us?"

"I already knew what you'd say," her mother replied.

"Yeah? But you did it anyway?"

"Someday you'll understand," Emma said weakly.

"I doubt it," Sis barked and stomped up to her room.

ten

F or two more weeks, it was just Bailey and Sis, getting up early, going out in *Leah Jean*, coming home with their catch, but something had gone out of it for both of them. Knowing that soon they would be sharing the boat with Booty, that for the first time *Leah Jean* would work without a Kraft aboard, was a wound. Bailey resented the thought of Booty's hand on *Leah Jean*'s tiller, Booty's cooler stuck under the deck where Orrin's and now his had been, a place of possession. He hated the idea that Booty would be seen piloting the *Leah Jean*. He almost hated Emma for her part in it, a breach of faith.

In defiance, Bailey hurried to feed Sis the knowledge it had taken him years to acquire. He showed her how to knot the eel into the trotline with two quick twists of thumb and forefinger that looped a clove hitch over the bait. He taught her to watch the wind, then to lay out a line in the lee of the land so the ripples wouldn't warn the crabs that they were closing on the surface as the trotline rose to the net. His hand over hers on the tiller, he taught her how to slide the boat gently around the end of a float so he could pick it up easily, then run along the line, keeping it close, but not so close that it fouled the boat's propeller, until they reached the other end where Sis would stop the boat, reversing for a moment, then shifting into neutral while he brought the other float and weight aboard. He pulled off the engine box and showed her the manifold, the water pump, the fuel line connections, and the piece of hose he had replaced the week before their father died. He taught her to navigate, to read the tide and current tables, then to see it in reality as they passed buoys, the flowing current raising folds of water against their sides. Sis drank it all in as though she had been thirsting for this her whole life. She questioned him, brought the chart book out, and made notes in her spiral notebook in the peculiar shorthand only she could decipher.

As she made notes, Bailey told her stories, the tales of their Kraft forebears that his father had told him—the time their Great-grandfather Kraft invited Great-grandmother Nettie out, her first and only time aboard, so he could propose while he was tonging; the time in January of 1842 that Ludlow Kraft capsized his log canoe loaded with oysters, dragged the boat ashore, bailed it out, then went back to retong all the oysters he had lost, working so hard his sodden clothes didn't have a chance to freeze (though he lost four toes to frostbite). If Sis noticed that women barely figured in the Kraft legend, she made no remark. Instead, she took down everything Bailey said, remembering, piecing together the family history, buoyed by the certainty that every Kraft was born with river water in their veins.

Booty stayed away. Bailey and Sis would pass him, following down the dock like Tud's shadow to and from *Evelyn Louise*, his head down, avoiding Bailey's eyes. If he had told Tud about his plans, Tud gave no indication. Neither did Booty until the day school started.

That morning, Bailey rose at 2:00 A.M. so they could be on the river when the state fishing rules allowed them to begin at 3:00. He anticipated loading the truck and then rousing Sis, but she was already in the kitchen making sandwiches and a thermos of coffee by the time Bailey came downstairs.

"I've got everything ready," she told him. Their school backpacks lay on the table, stuffed. "I've already packed our lunches. I'm making breakfast. I'll stick it in the cooler. Take those out to the truck and don't get anything slimy on 'em."

Three months ago, he would have resented her bossiness. Now, he saw it as collaboration. Nodding, he grabbed the backpacks, slung them both over a shoulder, and went out to load the truck. It was still dark by the time they were plowing through the sticky August air, bugs tattooing the windshield like rain.

"I been thinkin'," Bailey told her as they came down High Street and turned into Water Street toward the wharf. "We got to find a place to stick *Leah Jean* farther downriver or this won't work. We can't waste all this time gettin' to the oyster beds."

"Where?"

"Otto Snore's place," Bailey replied. "He and Grampa Kraft were old friends. He might do it for me on that account."

Sis nodded agreement but kept her eyes on the road ahead as they pulled into Hanson's.

"No one's here yet," she observed.

"We've got to get down there in time to work and get back here and then get to school. I wish I'd thought about it before so I coulda stashed the truck farther downriver."

"We gonna make it to school on time?"

"I don't know," Bailey frowned. "It's okay to be late today—they never do anything much the first day, but we can't do it again. Mom's likely to sell the boat out from under us."

With a little thrill, Sis noted the "us"—a sign of partnership she had hoped for but not dared to expect. Smiling, she sat up taller in the seat, going over in her mind the loading routine so they would waste no time. As Bailey came to a stop in the parking lot, she pushed open the door and jumped out with their cooler in one hand. Trotting around to the truck bed, she yanked a stack of empty baskets out with her free hand and headed for the boat. It wasn't until they had nearly finished loading *Leah Jean* that they saw Booty coming down the dock, a cooler in his fist. Bailey looked up, frowning. He was about to say something to put Booty off, but Booty spoke first.

"I figured you needed to get in and out from farther downriver, so I left Pop's truck at Otto Snore's. I remembered he was a ol' buddy of your granpap's. Pop'll be madder'n a hornet when he finds out the truck's gone, but I asked Wilf Curlew to swing by and bring him down to *Evelyn Louise* today. I'll come with you this time and drop you both there so you can make it to school. You can swap his truck for yours on the way by here or take Pop's to school, and I'll trade back this afternoon. After that," he continued, hardly taking time to draw breath, "we can leave *Leah Jean* at Otto's. I asked him the other day, and he said it was okay."

He spoke quickly, fearful of what Bailey might say given a chance to interrupt. Booty was walking on eggs, desperate to make a life for himself, terrified this opportunity would destroy the one friendship he treasured most in the world. Bailey looked at Booty, at the open face and kind eyes that he had known and trusted his whole life. He remembered Booty's long-ago offer to split his reward, sight unseen. The reward turned out to be a tour of the marine biology lab, not what either had hoped, but interesting and shared.

"Climb aboard."

Bailey reached down and cranked the engine to life as Booty cast off.

"I almost missed you," Booty said finally as they rounded Fryingpan Point. "I knew you'd be up and out early, but I didn't think you'd haul yourself out in the middle of the night."

Bailey smiled.

"Didn't figure we had a choice. How'd you get here from Tud's truck anyway?"

"Walked—and ran," Booty said matter-of-factly. "I got the feeling around 2:15 that I'd misjudged the time and you'd be here sooner than I figured. I'd kinda hoped to hitch a ride back in, but there weren't nobody much on the road."

Bailey's eyes opened wider.

"You musta left home at one," Bailey said, shaking his head.

"Earlier," Booty replied.

The three rode in silence until they reached the marsh near Bookers Wharf, where Bailey and Sis began setting out the line. Booty sat on the outboard coaming, watching. Instinct honed from years of dodging his father's moods told him to freeze, like an animal hiding in plain sight. He knew he was an intrusion.

Bailey was grateful he didn't have to talk save for the little snatches of instruction he gave Sis.

"Pay 'er out, now. . . . Hold up a little. . . . Okay, let 'er go some more."

He was beginning to feel the joy he knew his father once had in watching him learn. Though Sis kept her head down and her attention on the work, he could feel her excitement as the crabs began to come.

"I wasn't sure they would've waked up yet," Bailey confessed as they spun to make another pass.

"Just for you, Bailey." Sis grinned and darted a look at Booty, who remained silent, his face an amiable neutrality.

"Let's just hope it holds," Bailey responded.

Booty permitted himself the tiniest of smiles when he heard his friend's words, the beginning of forgiveness.

THEY DIDN'T MAKE it to school on time. Booty dropped Bailey and Sis off at Otto Snore's pier, rickety and hump-backed thanks to last winter's ice, its pilings like the legs of drunken storks. As soon as Bailey and Sis were off, he turned *Leah Jean*'s bow downriver without a backward look. Bailey watched for a moment as *Leah Jean* pulled away. He could see Booty draped against the overhead strut, his hand lightly caressing the tiller, every line of his body whispering familiarity, possession. Jealousy gnawed at Bailey's stomach, but he gripped the cooler tighter and turned away, heading up the uneven incline of the dock to Tud's old truck, which sat half on the edge of Otto's lawn under a huge old buttonwood tree.

They climbed in and Bailey twisted the ignition key. The starter rasped ineffectually against the solenoid. *It's not going to go*, Bailey thought. *Damn that Tud Warren. Why can't he ever have anything that actually runs?* He tried again, holding the key hard against its stop, listening to the starter until he could hear the battery begin to run down. He swore under his breath.

"We gonna make it?" Sis asked quietly.

Without answering, he tried one more time, pumping the accelerator and making anxious deals with his Maker under his breath. The engine caught and rumbled to life.

"Yeah," he muttered through clenched teeth. "We're gonna make it."

They had left their backpacks in their truck at Hanson's. Bailey had planned to swap trucks—he didn't want to chance dealing with Tud—but their usually reliable pickup wouldn't start. He hated leaving Booty with a problem and dreaded taking Tud's truck anywhere in case they crossed paths with Tud, but he had no choice. By the time he dropped Sis off at the elementary school in Bleeckerton it was nearly ten o'clock. *She'll catch hell*, he thought regretfully. *Maybe she can talk her way out of it.*

At the school office, he picked up his schedule and loped off to make the next class. He'd already missed English—a relief since he had struggled with it his entire school career—but he didn't want to miss biology. The natural sciences were his pleasure, his only real success. Yet he knew, even if few of his teachers did, that he wasn't a purely mediocre student. In some subjects, he had worked hard to get a C; in others, he had done just enough to maintain one. Any real effort and he would have sailed through with A's. Bailey had done it almost consciously. He wanted a little slack in his life. He didn't want people to expect too much.

But the natural sciences—the winds, the weather, the frogs and marshes, why the world turns the way it does—all made perfect sense to Bailey. One of the biggest thrills of his life had been peering for the first time into a microscope at a droplet of river water. Beneath the lens splatted on a little pane of glass, an entire world squirmed and throbbed, a world of living creatures and plants, a world he had daily let slide through his fingers unaware.

Mr. Lehman, a tall, slim man with fuzzy graying hair, was just coming to the K's when Bailey slid in the back door and took the last stool at a lab station.

"Bailey Kraft?"

"Here."

The teacher looked up for a moment, paused as though he was about to say something, then went back to the list. After class, Mr. Lehman stopped Bailey as he filed out with his classmates and put a hand on Bailey's shoulder.

"I was sorry to hear about your dad."

Taken off guard, Bailey felt his eyes fill with tears, and he gulped before managing to get "thanks" out of a constricted throat. He started to bolt, not caring why this virtual stranger had needed to express his sympathy—and shatter Bailey's equilibrium—but Mr. Lehman gently restrained him.

"Your dad was good to me when my father died. I was . . ." Mr. Lehman cleared his throat and started again. "He let me come out on the *Leah Jean* with him for a while. It helped."

Bailey nodded, not trusting his voice to speak and not knowing what to say.

"Do you still have her?" Mr. Lehman pursued.

Bailey nodded again, not adding the *sort of* that popped into his mind.

"Well, I just wanted you to know that I thought a lot of your dad. And if there's anything I can do . . . ," he trailed off.

"Thanks."

Suffocating, Bailey longed to escape to the river, where he could breathe again.

"I'm looking forward to having you in my class," Mr. Lehman said, smiling.

"Thanks," Bailey repeated, eyes on the floor. "I . . . I gotta get to my next class."

"Sure. See you later."

That afternoon, Bailey waited for Sis in the elementary school parking lot, anxious to meet Booty at Hanson's rather have him come to the house to trade vehicles, an attempt to excise Emma from anything to do with the boat. He drove through town, humiliated at Tud's roaring muffler, but their truck was gone by the time they pulled in the parking lot. They got out and walked down to the end of the dock where *Leah Jean* sat contentedly at the end of her mooring lines.

"He's scrubbed her down," Bailey noted, almost to himself.

"He thinks it's his," Sis muttered.

Bailey didn't contradict her, wondering if Sis was right or if Booty was only trying to show Bailey he'd make a good partner and to make up for his underhandedness in taking a part of the boat away.

"Let's get back to the house in case he brings our truck back. Don't want to keep him waitin'," Bailey said.

The two rode in silence, each wondering how Booty's day had been, what kind of catch he had had without a Kraft on board. Sis hoped he would come up empty-handed, evidence that no Warren could touch the Krafts. Part of Bailey wanted the same thing. But another part, one that had watched Booty struggle all his life with discouragement and loss, wanted him to do well. And the better Booty did, the better they did—at least for now.

Their truck was in the driveway by the time they clattered to a stop behind it. Booty was unloading the bait into the brine barrel.

"How'd ya do?" Bailey asked, despite his internal promise that he wouldn't.

Booty shrugged.

"Not too bad. I got three more bushels after you left."

Bailey's eyebrows went up. Not bad. Really good, in fact.

"I gave your ma your split."

Bailey stiffened. Booty noticed, turning away to settle the wooden top on the brine barrel as he spoke.

"It was her I made the arrangement with."

"Yeah."

Booty jammed his hands in his pockets, slid out the shed door past Bailey, and crossed the driveway to Tud's pickup.

"*Leah Jean* look okay?" he asked as he put his hand on the door.

"Yeah." Bailey replied, refusing to give the compliment he knew Booty was fishing for.

Booty nodded, climbed in, and started the engine.

"What time shall I meet you at Otto's?" he asked, his face closed as tight as an oyster.

"Eight," Bailey replied.

"Good enough."

Booty backed Tud's truck out of the driveway, threw the old gearshift into forward, and roared off down the road.

eleven

&

For four days, they made it work despite the uneasy peace between them, but Bailey dreaded that first Saturday. Saturdays had belonged to him and Orrin. Every year, once school was in session, Bailey wasn't allowed out on the boat during the week. Orrin had always said the weekdays were for his studies, uninterrupted. But Saturdays were different. Bailey needed the river, and his father knew it. Saturday—together—was renewal; it sustained them both. Now, Bailey would still be out on Saturday, could still draw peace from the river's lilting voice, whispered in her eddies and ripples and the swoosh of the ospreys' wings, but without his father it was incomplete, diminished.

And while he dreaded being without Orrin, he didn't want Booty there. Booty, who had never asked anything from him but friendship, who had never pushed, was pushing now. Bailey needed time to adapt to this new arrangement, this new Booty. He needed at least one day a week out there alone, to reestablish his connection with the water and with *Leah Jean*, to renew his knowledge of her groans and creaks, her response to his touch on the tiller. He might be forced to share her with someone else, but he wanted to know that she was still really his.

He knew Emma would fight him on this, but he was convinced he could win this time. One day a week. That was all he asked of her. His mother used to listen to him, respect his reasons. She would again. That first Saturday, he was working quietly, trying not to make noise, shoving baskets and bait into the truck bed, when she stopped him.

"Booty's going with you."

This wasn't the way he wanted this conversation to begin.

"Mom, I've done everything you ever wanted," he said, measuring his words, carefully walking the line between begging and demanding. She opened her mouth to speak, but Bailey kept going. "This is one thing I want. To be out on *Leah Jean* without anyone else. I took Sis out, taught her, looked out for her. . . ." He hesitated as the picture of Sis retching on the deck after he had rescued her flashed through his mind, but he went on. "I'm in school like you want, home for supper. I've done everything you've asked and been right where you've wanted me to be. Every time. Mom, I . . ." He started to say *need this*, but stopped. "I'm due."

A look of compassion flashed across her face, but Emma shook her head.

"Booty's our partner now—at least he's workin' in that direction— and he's goin' with you."

"The hell he is," Bailey said.

"Watch your mouth, Son," she snapped. "I don't want you going out alone. There's an end of it."

"You don't seem to mind if Booty goes out alone," Bailey retorted. The inequity turned a thumbscrew on his sense of fairness and made him feel as though she didn't trust him.

"Whether I mind about Booty or not is another matter. He's not my son," she replied with a logic that Bailey found impossible to follow.

He knew she cared for Booty, had looked after him—in many ways like a mother—since Lottie had left. But he realized her love for Booty lacked the fierceness of her feelings for him, her only son; yet she had bestowed a greater respect on Booty with this single, vital, division of privileges.

"I'm going without Booty whether you like it or not!"

"You know I could—" She stopped.

Both knew what she was about to say. *I could sell the boat.* End of argument. It was coercion and he hated her for it. She hated herself for it, too. But she was desperate to keep what she had left.

So Bailey and Booty went out together on Saturdays. At first, it was silent, angry running the entire time. Chewing on a resentment he couldn't swallow, Bailey spat it out at Booty, barking orders, letting Booty know that in the truest sense, the boat would never be his, no matter how much Booty paid or how many years he fished it.

At the end of September, they gave up crabbing and started tonging for oysters. Sis wanted to learn, but she was too small to manage even the short, twelve-foot tongs. Besides, Bailey didn't want her standing on the narrow deck in the dark. Even with a life jacket on, he didn't want her going into the water. He didn't want his mother to have any excuse to sell the boat outright—or to keep Sis from going out with him. Though he would not have admitted it, he needed her, wanted her with him on those dark mornings.

Mostly, he and Sis worked together in silence, lost in their own thoughts, fighting both the seeping cold and the growing urge to give it all up. But Sis rarely complained. And she was getting good at culling, sorting the keepers that met the legal size requirements from the ones that were too small and had to be thrown back for next year or the year after. Even with her small hands enveloped in oversized rubber gloves, an awkward but effective protection against the razor-edged shells, she was good.

As a benchmark for measuring oyster shells, Bailey had renotched the culling board, the wide wooden trough that lay across the stern where he dumped each clutch of oysters he brought up; it was the same notch Orrin had cut for him when he was young and couldn't eyeball them.

FALL ABBREVIATED THE days and sucked the green out of the landscape. The reeds and grasses faded, verdure sliding out as though being drunk down by the river itself, leaving only colorless stalks bending their heads to whisper secrets, then shushing each other in the wind. The once green farm fields were now swaths of fawn-colored feed corn or unpicked soybeans, and the trees along the shore were blotched with color.

Bailey and Sis were working in the dark nearly all of the time now. Except for Saturdays, Booty got all the daylight. The lack of sleep and the surreal feeling of wandering around all night long were wearing on both of them. Now Sis came aboard each morning and crawled into a bunk for another hour's sleep while Bailey motored to an oyster bed and began to work. Standing on the gunwale with one long handle of the tongs in each hand, like a posthole digger, scissoring, scissoring until his arms and back and neck ached, he worked like a robot until it was time to meet Booty. Once they had traded places, Bailey and Sis, tired before the day began, set off for school.

It was hard. But even harder was the battle against the memories of Orrin and their life before his death that intruded and destroyed what little internal peace Bailey managed to build. His guilt over Orrin's death had begun to dissolve, but in its place he was discovering anger, a cold, hard fury at his father's leaving—and at his denying Bailey his rightful inheritance, the one thing that would have consoled him. The *Leah Jean*.

As Bailey took the boat out, he wondered how long they could keep this up. Sis had been true to her word; her first grades were, as usual, nearly perfect. But there were dark circles under her eyes, and she collapsed into bed every night right after supper. Emma hadn't objected—yet. But Bailey worried that it was only a matter of time.

When he cut the engine, Sis stirred. A true waterman, Bailey thought admiringly.

"Time, Sis," he called softly, unwilling to pierce the river's quiet with a shout.

Without a word, Sis rose and dragged herself out to the stern. Bracing a flashlight on the culling board between two oysters, she began working in the yellow pool of its beam. She moved mechanically, bulky in her foul-weather gear and life jacket. She set to work on the mound of oysters that Bailey had already pulled up, dumping the keepers in a bushel basket at her feet, and chucking the undersized ones overboard in the opposite direction from where Bailey tonged so he wouldn't bring them back up again.

At 7:15, Bailey cranked up the engine and headed back up the river toward Otto Snore's. Sis poured herself a cup of coffee, thick with cream and sugar, and came to sit by Bailey on the engine box. A gossamer mist cloaked the river, obliterating the few lighted buoys, but Bailey, unperturbed, chugged along at full speed. Sis sipped at the coffee, hands cupped around its warmth.

"Stewie Bevins said I smell like fish," she announced.

"Stewie Bevins is a asshole," Bailey replied automatically, then looked down at his sister and saw the tears standing in her eyes.

"He's not the only one," Sis said, the quiver in her voice apparent even over the noise of the engine.

"Asshole?"

"No! He's not the only one who says I smell like fish."

Bailey thought about it for a moment.

"Wash up in the girls' room before class," he suggested.

Sis shook her head. "It doesn't help. I tried."

Bailey wanted to say forget 'em all, but he knew it wasn't an option for Sis. Her personal image had always been important to her; from the time she was old enough to walk and talk, she had cared what others thought. Bailey had always had the river. And Orrin.

"Perfume?"

Sis shook her head again.

Bailey hesitated a moment before asking, "What do you think you should do?"

He prayed she wouldn't say stop. Stop struggling every morning, stop trying to do it all, stop trying to hang onto what was slipping out of their hands. Just stop. And rest. The possibility of her leaving lay like a weight on his chest. He needed her company and her help. Without her, he was afraid it was finished.

After what seemed an eternity, Sis shrugged. Hunched into a ball over the remains of the coffee, which had begun to revive her a little, she looked up at her brother. "I don't know. I just want 'em to stop sayin' mean things."

"I'll come tromp all over 'em," Bailey grinned in relief. "How's that?"

"Just Stewie," Sis said, mustering a smile in return.

"Okay," Bailey agreed. "I'll just tromp Stewie."

Booty met them on the dock at eight, cooler in hand. They traded places wordlessly, like sentries changing watch. Dawn reached purple and rose-colored fingers across the remains of the night sky and began to butter the treetops with gold. Sis and Bailey climbed into their truck and lumbered off down the road while Booty took the boat back down the river. Bailey glanced back over his shoulder at the boat, unaware that what he felt was the ache of a jealous lover. He glanced over at Sis, tucked into a ball against the passenger's door like an exhausted soldier, mentally bracing for combat with her uninitiated classmates.

Elizabethtown glowed pink as Bailey swung out onto Route 20 and turned toward Bleeckerton, finally pulling up—against the rules—in front of the school to let Sis out. She shed her foul-weather gear, then grabbed her backpack off the floor.

"Tell Stewie I'll come gunnin' for him if he makes any more cracks about you," Bailey told her.

"Yeah," Sis smiled wanly.

She hauled her things out of the truck, kicked the door shut, and trudged off to class.

As Bailey swung back out of the parking lot, he saw in the rearview mirror one of the teachers shouting and motioning for him to stop—

probably going to object to how, or when, he had dropped Sis off—but he pretended not to see her. The two parking lots, elementary and high school, were nearly adjacent, but to get to the high school he had to go out onto the road, turn onto Route 298, then turn back into the entrance and over the speed bumps, adding another five minutes to his time. He slid into his first period class—English—just as the teacher closed the door.

Bailey struggled with English. He had trouble not just with the reading and the maze of conflicting ideas the teachers wanted students to draw from all those novels they assigned but with the language itself. The way he was used to hearing words strung together bore only a passing resemblance to the rules of grammar by which school papers were judged. It was one reason Sis did so much better than he did in school. Somehow—a musical ear he had overheard someone say—she picked up and clung to the kind of English the people on Water Street spoke, "upper class" in his mind. But while it subtly set her apart, it also helped her. She's the one should go to college, Bailey thought.

At lunch, huddled over the peanut butter and jelly sandwich Sis had made for him, nearly asleep in the warm, buzzing cafeteria, he considered the idea of trading his own college education for one for Sis. Emma just might buy it, he thought. Then he could stay on the river. He didn't realize he had dozed off until Sarah pushed the arm he had propped his chin on out from under him and he nearly fell into what remained of his lunch.

"Hey, Bailey. Don't you speak to people any more?"

"Hey, Sarah."

He tried to pull to mind the last thought he had had before drifting off, but it was gone.

"You look terrible, Bailey," Sarah informed him. "Are you gettin' any sleep?"

Bailey tried to glare at her, but he didn't have the strength. Instead, he poked aimlessly at the remains of his sandwich.

"Not much," he confessed.

"Are the oysters good this year?" she asked changing tacks.

"Yeah. Bunch o' selects this mornin'."

"Good. I hear Sis is goin' out with you every day."

Sarah didn't say she had skipped class one day to corner Sis on the elementary school playground and bombard her with questions about Bailey. Sis, feeling protective of their tenuous hold on daily living, had not bothered to tell Bailey.

"Yeah. She's a good culler."

"She like it?"

Bailey thought a minute and realized he had never asked. Sis had insisted on coming, had joined his plan—her plan really, he had to admit to himself, if not to Sarah—to keep the boat and keep going, but he didn't know, now that things were getting to be a slog through cold weather and darkness, now that the exhaustion of nonstop work was wearing them down, if she liked it or simply endured. But then again, did it matter? They could do this. They had known it would be hard. There was no turning back.

"Yeah, she likes it," Bailey replied.

"Well, you both look like you been run over," Sarah told him.

"I gotta go," Bailey started to rise, but Sarah snatched at his sleeve.

"What're you gonna do for Thanksgiving?"

"Thanksgiving? That's . . ."

"Ten days."

"Oh." The days had been like uniform beads strung on a looped cord, one nearly indistinguishable from the next except for Sunday, the day when he collapsed into bed and stayed there half the day. "I guess I'll be goin' out oysterin' in daylight for a change," Bailey replied.

"Mom wanted to know if all three of you wanted to come to our house for Thanksgiving dinner."

Bailey shrugged, pushing aside the image of the empty place at their table this year.

"We've had Tud and Booty for Thanksgiving forever," he said. "I don't guess that's gonna change."

"I'm sure we could make room for them, too," Sarah said, trying not to appear too eager. She could feel him closing off from her, from everyone, into a world where no one could follow, save, maybe, Booty. And she wasn't about to let him go without a fight. She had loved him—sometimes with cause, sometimes irrationally—from the first moment she had set eyes on him in kindergarten.

"I'll call your mom," Sarah offered.

"Okay," Bailey replied, balling up the remains of his lunch.

Like a sleepwalker, he headed for the door and dumped the bag into the garbage without a backward glance. Even if he had looked back, he was too far away to see the tears standing in Sarah's eyes.

twelve

*the Saturday before Thanksgiving was clear. By nine, the sun glinted off glassy ripples in a thousand bright shards. *Leah Jean* slid past RN 18 with Bailey at the helm. Booty rarely touched the tiller when Bailey was aboard, though every day he grew more eager to assert his claim on her. He had spent his life trying to stay out of the way, to fit in as unobtrusively as possible. Now, for the first time in his life, he could taste ownership, a place over which he had legitimate claim; he wanted to mark the boat—and the work—as his own.

"It's gonna be a good day," Bailey observed, his nose in the wind.

Booty nodded and pulled his jacket closer.

"Chilly, though," he said.

"You always were too warmblooded," Bailey observed.

"Is it warmblooded or coldblooded?" Booty asked, hoping to crack open a door back into their friendship. "I thought that lizards were coldblooded, and they've gotta lie on rocks to keep warm."

"I don't know," Bailey shrugged. "If you're so all-fired interested, why aren't you still in school?"

Booty shrugged.

"What's the point? All I'm ever gonna be is a waterman."

"Whadaya mean *all*?" Bailey demanded. "That's a lot! Bein' a waterman's a hell of a lot. My English teacher read somethin' the other day that said, 'It's not fish you're buying—it's men's lives'!"

Booty smiled indulgently.

"Yeah? Seems to me lives come pretty cheap these days."

They stared at each other for a moment, each imagining the decisions and the possibilities that would shape their days and years.

"It'll get better," Bailey said, reassuring himself as much as Booty. "The fish'll come back. We just got low times right now."

"Maybe, maybe not," Booty shrugged again.

"If you don't think it's gonna get better," Bailey said, "then what're you doin' out here, huh? You could come ashore, join some construction company, make some real money. Anyone can learn to swing a hammer."

If he believed the whole thing was dying, Bailey thought, what was he doing trying to take *Leah Jean* away?

"Don't wanna," Booty grinned perversely.

"No? How come?"

Booty looked off across the river to where a single bald eagle soared above the leafless trees on shore, circling for her nest. Bailey might as well have asked him why, knowing that he would die one day, he bothered to breathe. Being a waterman was what kept Booty alive. The river was the only certainty in his life. He would not, no matter how bad it got, give it up.

"Because I love it," Booty replied, dropping his voice too low for Bailey to hear.

Seeing the answer written plain across his friend's face, Bailey turned away. He didn't want to pity or to understand. He only wanted his boat back.

Bailey slowed the boat, then threw it into neutral and watched as she slid gracefully to a near halt, dipping and sidling a little as her wake caught up to her. Looking across the sparkling blue river to the Chesapeake Bay, Bailey nodded to himself and stepped around the engine box toward the three sets of tongs that lay like giant chopsticks on the deck. Before he could reach them, Booty bent down and grasped the sixteen-foot tongs.

For a few uncomfortable seconds they locked eyes.

"I been usin' these all week," Booty said finally.

Deftly, he extracted them from the clawed baskets of the other two pairs, climbed up onto the port side deck, walked forward and slid the tongs into the water without a backward glance.

Furious, Bailey took up the twelve-foot tongs and threaded them out the opening between the overhead canopy and the stern. Moving forward, he took up his position on the starboard side and fed the tongs down as far as he could, waiting to feel the oysters beneath. The twelve-footers were too short to mine the depth of the bed. Bailey was forced to crimp himself in half just to touch the top layer of shells. He could almost feel oysters, a foot, two feet deeper, yet he could not get hold of them. Worse, he could hear the muffled scritch-scritch of Booty's tongs, metal rakes rasping over oyster shells, the top of a cache of fat bivalves that Bailey could nearly smell.

Booty dumped a hefty load onto the board, then swung the tongs back out and dropped them into the water to begin again while Bailey was still trying to fill his rakes. After a few more swipes, Bailey brought his tongs up, hand under hand, and swung their pitiful half-catch over the stern and onto the culling board. Seeing his small mound beside Booty's mountain rankled.

They pulled up a few more loads, looking from the stern like animated bookends, each broadening back bent over the water intently, shoulders and arms knotting and flexing, hips urging bodies along as, load by laborious load, they scraped their living off the bottom of the river. Drifting, *Leah Jean* bobbed gently, cradled between the freshening breeze and the duck-tailed waves.

The heaped oysters had begun to spill from the culling board onto the deck, their sharp, rippled edges gouging little divots out of the paint. The careless indignity to *Leah Jean* grated on Bailey. Booty, who had been brought up on a boat whose maintenance had been hurried at best, was oblivious.

"Why don't you cull while I find a new spot?" Bailey said with exaggerated casualness.

"Seems to me this spot's just fine."

Booty's huge mound of oysters dwarfed Bailey's, which gave him intense satisfaction. At the end of the day, they would split the profit without regard to how much each had pulled aboard, so it made no difference who brought up more. But for once in his life, Booty was winning and he wasn't about to give that up.

"Don't want to play her out," Bailey said, furious at having to negotiate what he believed should have been his to command.

"I'm bringin' up more," Booty replied as he released a load. "How 'bout you cull a while and I'll spell ya when my back gives out."

The two friends stood for a moment, territorial challenge in every line of their bodies. Bailey debated scrambling over the dewy top of the canopy and snatching the tongs out of Booty's hands, but he wasn't certain that, even propelled by anger, he would win. Instead, he came down the deck, fed the twelve-footers back into the slot between the engine box and the tiller, and took up his old position at the culling board. After pulling on gloves, he began sorting the keepers from the small fry. They worked for a half an hour more in bitter silence, Booty loading the culling board with mud-tarred oysters and Bailey culling angrily.

Finally, Booty straightened and worked one fist into the small of his back.

"Ready to move?" he asked Bailey.

"Yeah, I guess." Bailey's tone was studied, deliberate, as though he might, if he chose, decide to nullify Booty's suggestion, reclaim the longer tongs, and relegate Booty to the culling board.

Slowly, he finished culling the load on the board, making Booty wait. When the board was finally cleared, he pulled off the gloves, dropping them onto the board, then started the engine and threw the

gearshift into forward. Like a spooked colt alarmed at the unaccustomed tension of her rider, *Leah Jean* jumped ahead, digging her stern
down into the water. Booty, still standing on the narrow deck, grabbed
the handrail on the canopy to keep from going overboard. When they
had reached the open-water bend off Panhandle Point, Bailey slowed
her, then cut the engine, once again letting the boat drift to a stop.

"I don't think there's gonna be too much here," he said, with what
he hoped was authority, "but we can try."

"I did pretty well here the other day," Booty told him.

The contradiction grated.

"Let me have those sixteen-footers," Bailey barked.

"Sure," Booty said, satisfied that he had won his point. "I'll use the
ol' back breakers a while."

The wind was kicking up. Thick, gray-white clouds began to fill the
sky, blotting out large patches of blue and dropping the temperature
another ten degrees, but Bailey, forehead speckled with sweat, shucked
his jacket onto the engine box and returned to work in sweater and
shirt. Chilled once he stopped tonging, Booty zipped his jacket closed,
tucked gloved hands under his armpits, and did a little toe-warming
dance, waiting.

Now in possession of the sixteen-footers, Bailey relaxed. Stepping
up onto the port gunwale, he fed the tongs down through the dark
water until her could feel the spot where they had been worn to velvet
smoothness over the year by his father's hands. This physical connection
with Orrin warmed Bailey. It was tangible continuity, confirmation of
the rightness of his being there.

This is where I belong, he thought. *If I've got to take on the devil himself as partner to stay here, then I'll do it.*

Skilled and fast at culling, Booty had time to watch Bailey. He saw
his friend's unconscious attention to the movement of wind and boat,
his listening, his silent responses, his communion with the river. Booty

understood the contentment of that wordless conversation, the answers that came unbidden from the depths, answers that seemed to evaporate on shore.

The two worked in silence, avoiding each other's eyes, focused only on the catch. There was no reason to expect it—no gust or wind shift or sudden lurch on a tanker's wake as it came rolling away from the shipping channel. For a moment after he heard the heavy, deep-toned *sploosh*, Booty thought it had been a fish leaping as it struggled to catch a smaller one for dinner. He turned toward Bailey to suggest they get out a line, but Bailey wasn't there. He strained to see into the cabin, then around the meager canopy. Bailey was gone.

Scrambling to the side, Booty looked down into the water, but all he could see was dark uniformity. The river had swallowed Bailey whole.

"Oh God, oh God, oh God," he muttered, a prayer of sorts, as he stripped off gloves and coat, then kicked off his boots.

"Why isn't he coming up? Where is he? Why isn't he coming up? Did he hit his head? Is he under the boat? How long can he hold his breath? He can't drown. He just can't."

Sockfooted, Booty leaped over the side and crashed into the water. It was like hitting a stone slab. But once penetrated, the wall became liquid, seeping into clothing and joints, the cold penetrating blood and bone. It wrapped freezing arms around him, squeezing out his breath, pushing against the heart that thudded in his chest. Terrified, blind in the darkness, Booty kicked and flailed, striking in all directions, pushing water out of his path, searching for something, anything, to grab and bring to the surface.

Bailey, stunned, at first couldn't figure out what had happened. One minute, he was watching the reflection of his booted toes in the water, contentedly working the tongs; the next he was in it. He could feel the cold against his skin, slowing his reactions. Unconsciously, he still held the tongs, now a neutral weight. His lungs began to swell, crying for air, yet his boots, like cement around his legs, dragged him down. A fish swam by, brushing fins against his face in the darkness. *What is it like to die?* Bailey wondered, tempted to succumb to the river's pull. *Will I see Grandpa Kraft and Dad and Great-great-grandpa Ludlow? And if I do, what will they say? What will I say to them?*

Frantically, Booty pawed through icy water, an image of Emma's face flashing through his mind, her horror and sorrow at yet another loss, her aching, unspoken blame. All the while, a tiny voice in his head warned, "Don't drown yourself trying to save a drowning man," but he ignored it and continued to grasp at emptiness. Then he touched something, a wood shaft, a tong. He grabbed at it. It resisted. He pulled harder, only to have it come away in his hand. Releasing it, he clawed his way up to the chill air. His face broke the water, mouth gaping. Air wouldn't come and for a split second, he thought he had forgotten how to breathe, that his lungs had collapsed. Then he choked, and his chest heaved. Desperately, he gulped in air and spray. Gagging, Booty spun around in the water, praying for a glimpse of Bailey's head above the river.

A second later, Bailey rose and broke the surface, like a loggerhead turtle hissing, sputtering, then more human, coughing. Hair plastered to his head, his face ashen and lips nearly purple, Bailey blinked and sucked down several deep draughts of air. Locating *Leah Jean*, who was making a sly, sideways getaway in the contradictory wind and current, he started for the boat, his sweater a watery vestment floating in slow motion around him. For a few seconds, watching Bailey's ghostly face, Booty half-wondered if his friend had died and was coming back to take him too, but the noise, the awkward splash and pull, rooted him to this earth and brought Booty back to reality. Alive. They were both alive. Four minutes, maybe five. That's all that stood between life and death, but they were still here.

Once he saw that Bailey was swimming, Booty pulled himself toward *Leah Jean* in a leaden-armed breaststroke. Panting, he struggled to take in air but could only draw down half-breaths, the cold water pressing against his diaphragm. Each time he drew closer, the boat seemed to move away. Come on, he urged himself, come on, you can't let her win. She's not going to desert you. Not this time. Come on, keep chasing. You'll catch her. He could feel his strength ebbing, then, as though she had reconsidered, *Leah Jean* halted and bobbed just a few feet from him. With his remaining energy, Booty kicked and swam toward her, finally managing to bring one arm out of the water and grab the port rail. Gasping, he turned, but Bailey had slowed. His movements were sluggish, half-hearted.

"Come on, dammit!" Booty shouted, through lips anesthetized by the cold. He couldn't leave the boat, his only sure salvation, to rescue Bailey. The attempt would take them both. His hands were like lumps of dough at the end of his arms, fingers barely able to grip. Emma's face swam before him.

"Come on, you sonofabitch!"

Bailey's head jerked.

"I'm gonna take your precious *Leah Jean* if you can't make it back," Booty cried, his voice so hoarse and slurred he wasn't sure Bailey could even understand him. "I'm gonna fish out the river and leave you to drown!"

Bailey kicked and grabbed handfuls of water to pull himself toward the boat.

"What's your Kraft kin gonna say when you get to those pearly gates—you let a Warren have the boat!" Booty bawled, goading him on.

Bailey willed himself forward, gasping like a landed bass, jaw chattering spasmodically. When he reached the side, he put his cheek up against the hull. Booty grabbed him by the shoulder. Covered in waterlogged sweater, drained of strength, his blood plodding through half-frozen veins, Bailey tried to reach the gunwale, but missed. Falling back, he submerged again, eyes wide just beneath the surface.

For a second, he thought he was going to drown in *Leah Jean's* shadow. Then he felt Booty pull again. With a strength he didn't know he had, Bailey kicked and brought one arm straight up and out of the water, narrowly missing Booty's face. This time, he managed to hook his hand over the rail. For one blessed and painful moment, Bailey hung there, working hard just to breathe, eyes closed.

Satisfied that Bailey was finally connected to the boat, Booty let go of his collar and grabbed the rail. Hanging there, face pressed against *Leah Jean's* slick topsides, his arms felt barely attached to his body, but he held on, talking to himself, urging himself on when he felt most like giving up—just as he had all his life.

It was a long pull. Not bad when every muscle is working with smooth reliability, but a matter of sheer will with blood slowed to molasses and hands almost too stiff to cling. Concentrating, Booty pistoned up out of the water once, twice, gaining confidence. The third time, he pulled with a roar and managed to hook his rib cage over the gunwale. Gasping as the rail dug into his ribs, he repositioned his hands and pushed, bringing his torso far enough over the rail to slither down onto the deck sodden and bruised. Purple veins stood out in sharp relief against the pale gray of goose-prickled skin shrunk against his bones.

Staggering to his feet, he went to the side and grabbed Bailey's free arm. Twisting his hand around, Bailey latched on in return. With their remaining strength, they pulled, each toward the other, until Bailey rose up out of the river and was draped over the coaming, gasping. Icy water ran off him in rivulets. Booty took hold of Bailey's pants, like a load of potatoes or the catch of his life, and hauled him in. Bailey folded into a heap on the deck, convulsed with cold. Booty went to the cabin, slapping sodden stockinged feet against the slippery deck, and retrieved two disintegrating foul-weather jackets from the hook near the companionway. He wrapped them around Bailey, then pulled on his own sweater and jacket, grateful for the shield against the rising wind. Rubbing his hands together, he reached for the starter.

"Don't leave those tongs," Bailey rasped, clawing his way to the side to peer into the water.

"The hell with the tongs!" Booty cried, as the engine rumbled to life.

"The hell with that!" Bailey dragged himself up to search harder. "There they are!"

"I don't see 'em," Booty growled, throwing it in gear. "We gotta get in before we get too cold to move."

"Over there, damn it! Over there!" Bailey insisted. He wasn't about to leave those tongs, with the imprint of Orrin's hand worn so indelibly on their shafts.

Following Bailey's glazed stare, Booty saw the tips of the tongs, like two oversized corks bobbing in the waves about forty feet away. Jaw clenched, he swung the boat around and slid alongside them, then reached over, careful to hang onto the gunwale, and pulled them aboard.

"A fine thing if I drowned trying to bring the damned tongs aboard!" he snarled, shoving past Bailey to fling them back on the pile.

"You won't drown gettin' those tongs," Bailey snapped, huddled nearly beneath the coaming. "But you might have goin' in after me. What the hell did you think you were doin'?"

Booty turned on Bailey, his mouth wide in disbelief.

"What?"

"I said," Bailey rasped through teeth that chattered so hard his words were almost unintelligible, "what the hell do you think you're doin' goin' in after me?"

"And what the hell am I supposed to do?" Booty shouted.

"You're supposed to stay aboard and pull me out when I come up instead of leavin' the boat. That was a stupid thing to do."

Too furious even to look at Bailey, Booty flung the throttle wide open, despite the rattled protest of the engine, and swung the boat in a narrow arc. She dug her shoulder down into the waves and turned obediently for home.

Unable to stand, Bailey crawled into the cabin. His fingers felt like glass, stiff and fragile as he struggled to pull off his wet clothes and wrap himself in the Swiss-cheese blanket that Orrin had years before snatched from Emma's Goodwill pile. It wasn't much, but it felt a whole lot better than the river. Bailey was furious with himself—he felt like a fool for falling overboard—but he was more angry at Booty for being the one to come in after him, for trying to save him. Krafts saved other people. They didn't need saving. The solid truths of his life were dissolving and running through his hands.

Booty stood by the tiller, shoulders hunched, one gloved hand tucked under his arm, the other on the tiller, his anger surging. He had gone in after Bailey and then nothing. No thanks, no acknowledgment, nothing. Nothing but those damned tongs. The Kraft tongs. The Kraft pride. Booty hadn't realized until that moment how deeply Bailey's pride had cut into their friendship.

Booty slid *Leah Jean* to a graceful halt at Otto's dock, dropping the permanent mooring lines onto their cleats. Toes throbbing with the cold, he began to unload the day's catch. He had balked at the tongs, but he would have lost all his toes before he left the oysters to die. Wasting the river's gifts meant they'd be grudgingly bestowed next time.

Bailey, still wrapped in the blanket, awkwardly picked up another basket and struggled after him. Once the boat was unloaded and locked up, the two of them climbed in the truck with Booty, by unspoken agreement, at the wheel. Bailey's fingers were like sausages as he fumbled with the heater, flapping at the dials. Its initial blast of cold air felt fiery on their freezing limbs. Bailey's body had begun to ache by the time they reached town, and his muscles were putty.

Booty unloaded the truck at Hanson's, collected their money, and drove Bailey home. His wet clothes were now a clinging second skin, the money a wad of damp bills in one pocket. After screeching to a halt in the driveway, he jumped out and slammed the door behind him, went up the steps and into the empty house. He stomped through the mudroom to the kitchen where he slammed Emma's take for the day onto the table, then turned and clattered back out. He passed Bailey, who was just stumbling out of the truck.

"How're you gettin' home?" Bailey asked.

"Whadda you care?" Booty growled without turning around.

He stalked out onto the road and set off on foot for home.

"Fine," Bailey muttered, pulling his stiff body up the back steps and into the house.

Standing in a tepid shower, his toes and fingers pulsing, blood-red and raw, guilt gnawed at the edges of his mind. He knew that Booty's impulse to go after him was born of an unquestioned friendship. And somewhere in the pit of his stomach, he knew he had ground it under a prideful heel; yet he needed Booty to be wrong. *Booty shouldn't have gone in*, he insisted to himself. *It's one of the first rules. If we'd both been drowned, it would have been Booty's fault.*

By the time Emma and Sis got home, he had stuffed his wet clothes into the dryer and set them to tumble for an hour. He had hoped to have them out before his mother found them—the fewer reasons she found to question him the better—but she came hustling into the house and, after dropping two bags of groceries onto the kitchen table, opened the washer and started to switch the finished load to the dryer.

"What's this?" she demanded as Bailey came in dressed in worn sweat clothes.

"What? Oh, it was blowing out there today. They got real wet," he lied, hoping his face wouldn't give him away.

Emma studied him for a moment but declined to challenge. Instead, she pulled the sweater and pants, warm but still damp, from the dryer and replaced them with the clotted contents of the washing machine.

"You should have washed it first," she said. "The dryer probably stinks of the river."

"Sorry."

"How'd you and Booty do?" she asked, her back to him.

"He left you your share on the table. Didn't you see it?"

"Yeah. I saw it. I mean, how are you doing together?"

"Why?" he asked, unaware that he had physically recoiled from the question.

Emma straightened. Her eyes looked faded, shrunk into the dark circles around her eyes.

"Because it's me you're mad at, and I don't want you to take it out on him."

"What makes you think I'm not mad at him, too?" Bailey shot back. "You would've never thought to sell *Leah Jean* if he hadn't come to you. She should be my boat and you know it!"

Emma sighed.

"Bailey—"

"No! You can't make this right! It's none of your business about me and Booty, so just stay out of it."

He turned and accidentally jammed his shoulder into the door frame before going through the kitchen and up to his room, where he slammed the door with such force that it reverberated through the house.

"What's goin' on?" Sis demanded.

"Nothing," Emma said, slamming the door on the dryer and punching the ON button before returning to the kitchen.

"What'd you say to Bailey?"

"Nothing. Now leave it alone!" her mother snapped, pulling a bag of carrots out of a paper bag.

Sis stood for a moment, debating whether or not to pursue her mother—she could be relentless when she felt that the stability of her own life was at stake—but decided her mother was closed to discussion, for now anyway. Instead, she pulled a box of cookies from the bag, tucked it under her arm, and took the back stairs two at a time to Bailey's room.

At the closed door, Sis hesitated, then knocked softly.

"Go away!"

She put her face close to the door.

"It's me, Bailey. Let me come in."

She waited. Finally, taking the silence for acceptance, she turned the knob and pushed open the door. Bailey lay spread-eagled across the bed on his back, glaring at the ceiling. Sis tiptoed in and sat on the edge of the bed. Opening the cookies, she pulled one out and handed it to Bailey, who took it and stuffed it whole into his mouth.

"What's goin' on?" she asked when he had swallowed.

"Nothin'."

"I'm sick of 'nothing' for an answer," she complained, taking a bite of cookie and handing him another. "What's going on?"

Bailey bit this one and stared hard at the ceiling as he chewed.

"Booty's changing."

"How?"

He shrugged.

"I don't know. He's actin' . . ."

"Like it's his boat?"

He nodded.

"Yeah."

"Told ya."

He shot her a look that was the next best thing to a slap and pressed his lips together.

"What's with the clothes?"

"Whaddaya mean?" he feigned ignorance.

"It wasn't that windy out there today, was it?"

"What do you know about it?" he demanded. "You been out there a few months and now you're a expert? Screw you!"

Six months ago, Sis would have made straight for their mother to tattle on Bailey. Now, she waited, watching him.

"I went overboard," he said finally. He wasn't about to tell even Sis that Booty had tried to save his life. Besides, it turned out not to be necessary. It was a wrong decision on Booty's part and an unwaterman-like thing to do.

Sis's eyes narrowed. "What happened?"

"Nothing happened," he snapped, then relented. "I went in; I got out. That's it. No big deal."

"Was it freezing?"

"It wasn't warm," he acknowledged.

"Wow," she breathed, imagining her brother, her only link to their father and their family history, gone. Another chunk of their lives obliterated. "What'd Booty do?"

"Whaddaya mean, what'd Booty do?" Bailey muttered. "He did what he was supposed to do."

Sis eyed him suspiciously.

"So when did it happen? Did you have a chance to get much?"

"Some."

Munching meditatively, Sis leaned back on the bed and looked out the window.

"Sarah stopped me today."

Bailey darted her a look, but said nothing.

"She wants us to come to her house for Thanksgiving."

"She told me."

"I said we always had Tud and Booty here."

"That's what I told her."

"She said they could come."

"Why doesn't she talk to Mom? She's the one who arranges holidays."

"Sarah wants you to want to come."

Bailey leveled a gaze at her; she looked a little fuzzy around the edges. Warm, ensconced in the safe haven of his room, he could feel himself drifting.

"All I want is *Leah Jean* back."

"I know."

thirteen

Sarah cornered him at lunch on Monday.

"You're coming to our house on Thursday."

"Okay," Bailey said without inflection.

Last summer, that would have made his heart leap. Now, it was just another thing to do, to find the time and energy for.

"I can't make it early. I'll be out."

"Your mom said you weren't going out on Thanksgiving Day."

"She's wrong," Bailey sighed.

"Oh." Sarah thought for a few minutes and looked across the cafeteria to where a group of sophomore girls laughed together at some shared joke. "What time do you think you'll be in?"

Bailey shrugged. "I don't know. Three, maybe four. I won't have to get up at the crack of dawn since there's no school."

Sarah nodded.

"You couldn't take off one day?"

He shook his head. He couldn't explain to her—he could barely articulate it to himself—the battle he was waging for his manhood, his own self-respect. He took a bite of sandwich and chewed, glancing once at the clock. *Don't have my English homework*, he thought. *Maybe he won't call on me.*

"Booty and his dad are invited."

Bailey looked at Sarah but didn't respond. Although he didn't relish the thought of sitting at a strange table for the first Thanksgiving without his father, if they were at Sarah's at least he wouldn't have to see his mother—or worse, Tud—sitting in his father's chair.

"Are they comin'?"

"I . . . yeah, I think so. Mom invited 'em. Why?"

"Nothin'."

"What is it, Bailey?"

"Nothin'," he said again.

"You're getting to be impossible to talk to, Bailey Kraft," she said.

"Then why do you want me for supper?" he asked.

"Darned if I know!" she snapped, scooping up her lunch and striding across the cafeteria to flop down next to a small knot of senior girls.

Bailey had known from the moment he met Sarah's mother that she thought he was beneath Sarah—or should have been. But Sarah was stubborn. Once she decided someone was a friend, it took a lot to change her mind. Even so, though Sarah knew his house well and had stopped by to see his family regularly over the years, he had rarely been to Sarah's house. Once two winters ago when the river had frozen and the watermen were unable to go out, he had gone out skating with her and several of her friends, then come home with her for hot cocoa. Her father, a lawyer in town who had twice run for judge—and lost to a more popular but less qualified candidate—had been cordial enough, not warm, but at least not openly hostile. But when Orrin had come in his pickup to collect Bailey, her mother had been barely civil.

It said something for Sarah's powers of persuasion that she had not only convinced her mother to invite the waterman's widow and kids but Tud and Booty, too. It would be awkward to say the least. Had Booty told Tud about what happened last Saturday? Probably not. They were hardly speaking.

Bailey dreaded sitting at the table with Booty. At least at home, no one would have to pretend to get along. But more important was that they would be closer to Orrin. His spray-rimed jacket still hung on the back of the door; his pipe, its loamy scent still permeating the house, remained on the table by the lounge chair he used to fall asleep in at night. Those things, tangible proof of his existence, would bring him back to them a little, give him a presence at the table. At Sarah's, without those bits of evidence, Orrin was erased.

Despite his reluctance, Bailey knew why Sarah wanted him there. Part of him wanted to be with her, too. They were coming down to the end of high school. Time to make some decisions. Sarah was talking about going to the community college for a year—much against her mother's wishes since Sarah should by rights be going to some private college, maybe even Hopkins, her father's alma mater. She was smart enough and they had the money. But Sarah spoke only of her first year easing into the college life, staying close to home and family. While Bailey didn't acknowledge it, he understood it was also to stay close to him.

Bailey knew he loved her. And although he rarely showed it these days, Sarah had known it ever since they were children, when he had chosen her for his team on the playground even before the boys, when at ten he had sat with her at the back of the funeral home after her grandmother died and she had been too afraid to approach the open coffin, and when in seventh grade he had crossed the room to get her to come see the miracle of life that squirmed on the slide of river water in seventh grade biology. His feelings for her then had been less complicated, less filled with portent. But somewhere in eighth grade, when the boys and girls started pairing off, then bragging about what they did with and to each other, things began to change. Bailey had begun to draw back from her, go silent.

Sarah, who could feel his desire for her, couldn't understand the wall he had built, especially not after that kiss. Bailey had only kissed her once, last year, in an unguarded moment when she had come to the house and no one else was there. She had come up behind him as he stood in the mudroom, stripped to the waist and still wet from scrubbing off after mowing the lawn, and slowly traced the outline of a large bruise on his back with her finger.

"What'd you do now?"

Instead of answering, he had turned and caught her wrist in his left hand. Startled, she froze for a second, then put her hand against his face. For the first time in months, maybe years, the guarded look in his eyes had vanished. The warmth of his lips against hers sent an electrical thrill through her. Starved for his touch, she had leaned in and pressed her body against his, feeling the lean muscle, his thighs warm against her even through his jeans. With a flood of pleasure and relief, she realized he had reached both hands around her back and ran them from her shoulder to her flanks, gently, insistently exploring each curve and hollow. Pressed against him, she felt him harden, and wondered in one panic-stricken moment whether she would resist if he led her toward his bedroom. She wanted this and, at that moment, she didn't care about consequences. But he had stopped abruptly, gasping for air, and turned away toward the sink. Putting his head under the faucet, he turned on the cold water for a few seconds then, turning off the taps, reached around her to grab the towel by the door.

"We don't want to end up like Lizzie Smith and Buddy," he had said, pulling on his shirt.

"They don't love each other." Sarah, heart still pounding, nearly choked on the words.

He had looked at her, the tears standing in her eyes, her hands unconsciously clutched against her chest protectively.

"I won't ever make even half what your dad does, Sarah," he said.

"Do you think I care about that?"

"I care," he said softly.

She hadn't spoken to him for a month after that. In October, he had brought her a bushel of oysters, a waterman's gift. After that, she had begun to speak—in short, choppy, begrudging bursts at first, then easier, less strained. Eventually, she had returned to herself, chattering away about her schoolwork, the frustration of slogging through *Moby-*

Dick, planning a sleepover with friends. But it had never felt the same. Yet they were fixtures in each other's lives, constants, despite the ebb and flow of their emotions.

He sighed and looked over to where Sarah sat, head down, pretending to eat. Guilt stabbed him, but he didn't know how to approach her. An apology might open more doors than he could deal with. Better to leave it alone for now. He'd go out and bring an extra bushel of oysters back for Thanksgiving dinner. That might help with Sarah's mother. And Sarah would like it that he had tried, that he wasn't coming in empty-handed like some beggar.

Buying men's lives, he thought again. *They eat us up and throw away the shell.*

WEDNESDAY MORNING was sheet-metal gray and cold. The river looked faded, like an old photo negative, and smelled of snow, and the birds were silent, their energies spent in foraging for food. They had just changed crew. Sis had trudged up to the truck and folded herself into the cold cab, but Bailey stood on the dock watching Booty cast off.

"I'm takin' *Leah Jean* out with Sis on Thursday," he said. "We'll be back in time for supper."

Booty stared at him.

"What about me?"

"You get a day of rest. We'll be back in time for supper at Sarah's house. She said you and Tud're comin' too."

"Yeah."

"Well. That'll work out then."

Clamping his mouth shut, Booty walked forward to loop the mooring line onto the top of the piling, then went back and turned over the engine. He cast off the stern line, then slid the gearshift gently into forward. For one long moment, he looked at Bailey with such anger and reproach that Bailey had to look away. He wanted to say something,

something to excuse himself, to explain, to convince Booty that this had nothing to do with their friendship. But nothing came. Grimly, Booty pointed *Leah Jean*'s bow out into the channel. The outline of his shoulders, nearly as broad as Tud's, bowed as though beneath a yoke.

Bailey shuddered. He knew Booty would be angry about being kicked off on Thanksgiving, but he couldn't be on the boat with Booty again. Not so soon. The shame of that day, of his incompetence and pigheaded ingratitude, was too raw. And he needed to reclaim *Leah Jean*, to make her his own again. Booty will understand, he told himself. He always has.

Sis was balled up against the door when Bailey climbed in to drive them to school for the half day. Then a half day's rest. With a decent night's sleep, they'd be ready to go out tomorrow, glad to be on the water at dawn—hours after they had been getting up for nearly three months— a kind of renewal. And they'd return with a bushel of oysters for Thanksgiving. No charity for the Krafts. The weather report wasn't great, but its hit-and-miss accuracy was a long-standing joke among watermen.

But by the time Bailey woke the next morning, sleet tattooed the windows. It slightly dampened his enthusiasm, but he was determined to climb back aboard and restore his mastery. As long as it didn't blow too hard. After pulling on his thermal underwear and an extra pair of socks, he stole into Sis's room. She was spread out in crucifixion mode, arms draped across the bed, limp, with small, callused hands dangling over the sides. She had not been worried about monsters under the bed since Orrin had given her a baseball bat one night. "If you see any monsters," he had said to her, "you clonk 'em a good one and they won't come back." Bailey had listened outside and understood that Orrin was giving her a gift, the knowledge that she could take care of herself. Sis had slept with the bat in bed for a year, but now it stayed in the corner, just within arm's reach, a reminder of her father's love—and her own strength.

"Sis," Bailey whispered.

"What?" Sis lifted her eyebrows though her eyes were still glued shut.

"It's time," Bailey said, nudging her gently.

Sis reached up and opened one eye manually with thumb and forefinger, then turned toward the window.

"It's sleeting."

"Yeah," Bailey agreed, "but not too hard."

"I don't waaaanna," she moaned softly.

"Shhh! You'll wake Mom."

"Can't we take today off?"

"I don't want to go to Sarah's empty-handed," he insisted. "Besides, it'll be just like when Dad and I went out on Thanksgiving morning together."

Sis rolled back over on her back and peered at him through slitted eyelids.

"I miss him, Bailey."

"Me too. But out there, on *Leah Jean*, we're closer to him than anyplace else. It's like a visit with Dad, Sis. Just the two of us. We can just run down the river a little and get a couple bushels and come home. It'll be fun. Come on."

Sis sighed, stuffed her fists in her eyes, and rubbed hard.

"Is Booty coming?"

"No. I told him to take the day off," Bailey replied, feeling pricked with guilt.

"Okay. You go make coffee and something to eat. I'm tired of being cook."

Bailey lurched off the bed and tiptoed past his mother's open door and down the stairs. Passing through the kitchen, he went into the mudroom and switched on the overhead bulb, then went back into the kitchen to work in the half-light. Emma was a light sleeper and Bailey wasn't taking any chances. He had just finished making a thermos and sandwiches when Sis stumbled in.

"Grab your foul-weather gear and don't forget your life jacket," he said.

"It's on the boat," Sis muttered, pulling on a coat and dragging the foul-weather gear on over it.

Outside, Bailey opened the truck door carefully.

"Climb in and steer," he said softly. "I'm gonna push it down the driveway and a little away from the house so Mom don't hear."

"Bailey, I don't want to get in trouble."

"We won't," he insisted, impatient at her resistance. "Just get in."

Sis slid behind the wheel and grabbed it, but her gloves slid around it ineffectually. She pulled the gloves off and reluctantly took hold of the frigid wheel with bare hands.

"Put it in neutral," Bailey said, reaching around her to do it.

The truck drifted backwards into the road. He followed, sliding a little on the icy drive until it came to a stop. Opening the door, he snatched the ice scraper and chiseled an opening through the opaque layer that had built up on the windshield, then threw the scraper back into the cab. With Sis still at the wheel, he pushed the truck for a hundred feet, skidding on the slick roadway, then jumped in behind the wheel as it began to drift down the incline. He started the engine when they rounded the first curve.

"Are you sure we should be going out on a day like this?" Sis asked as they fishtailed around a turn.

"I had a great day with Dad one year when it was like this," Bailey assured her.

But he knew as he glanced at the bare-limbed trees bending and thrashing in the wind that it hadn't been like this. There had been virtually no wind that day. The sleet had come straight down, hitting the water with the singing peal of distant sleigh bells. Bailey, nine or ten and still small, had curled against the warm engine box, safely out of the freezing weather. The river was as unruffled as a big pond, but even so Orrin had tonged from the cockpit, not on the ice-clad deck. They were the only ones out that day, the only ones who dared. But Bailey had felt safe, ensconced in the mystery of the river and protected by the Kraft luck. That day as he tonged, his father had told stories about Krafts who went out in gales and returned with half again their limit—making up for the others who hadn't gone out—about Krafts who fell over and came back up as though thrust up by the river goddess herself, Krafts who faced the worst the river had to offer and won. Every time. That day, Bailey had felt invincible. Today would be the same, he told himself. But as he carefully navigated the icy road, glancing up at the treetops, he wasn't so sure.

Buckled into her seat belt, Sis strained forward, anxiously watching the slick road that wound and dipped like a gray satin ribbon before them.

"Look out! Slow down!" she cried as they skated around another corner. "I don't know Bailey. I bet no one's out today. It's awful."

"It'll be okay," he insisted, but his voice lacked conviction.

Sis cast a dubious glance his way, then returned her attention to the road, mentally guiding the truck around every curve and hollow. It had taken almost an hour to cover what normally took twenty minutes. Though he had maintained an impassive silence most of the way, as though concentrating on the driving, he had begun to calculate the danger. It wasn't like the day he had gone out with Orrin. Sleet was one thing. But the wind. Thirty-five he estimated, gusting to fifty and getting worse. You could tie yourself to the handrail, or tong from the cockpit to prevent sliding off an icy deck. But the wind, spraying the boat with layer upon building layer of ice. One list, one turn taken too sharply, and the boat would be over. He might have tried it with Orrin, or even Booty, but not with Sis. If anything happened, she wouldn't last ten minutes.

"I'll check the lines and then we'll see," Bailey said to Sis as they turned the last corner onto the road leading to the river. "I may have to buy a bushel to take to Sarah's."

Sis, rigid in the passenger's seat, visibly relaxed as they tooled down the fiord made by the tall trees on either side of the road. But at the end, Tud's ice-glazed truck rested nearly against the small bank, one front tire in the ditch.

He's checking the lines, Bailey told himself, irritated that Booty had beat him to it.

Bailey eased to a skidding stop, climbed out of the truck, and gingerly started down the dock. He struggled up the pier's hump-backed rise, gaining toeholds on the irregular slats, then skittered down the other side to the end. *Leah Jean* was gone.

"No!" Bailey wailed.

He squinted into the wind but could see nothing beyond the impenetrable curtain of sleet. The wind howled past his ears, shutting him in an insulated chamber of sound and cold.

"No!" Bailey hit his thigh with one balled fist.

Sis, who could only see the top of Bailey's head over the hump in the pier, opened the door and reluctantly slid out. Her foot skidded out from under her, and she grabbed the door handle to keep from sliding into the ditch. Regaining her balance, she stepped forward gingerly on the grass, better footing than the slick, crowned road. The ice-sheathed grass crumpled and broke beneath her feet. At the dock, she stopped and huddled against the wind, which cut swaths through the brittle reeds with the sound of shattering crystal. She waited, watching Bailey work his way back down the dock toward her.

"He's gone!" Bailey as he stepped off the dock.

"What do you mean gone?" Sis demanded.

"I mean, *Leah Jean* is gone, and Booty's gotta be the one who took her out."

Sis squinted across the reeds to the roiling river.

"Alone?"

"Tud'd never go out in weather like this."

Sis crimped her eyes against the sleet that needled sideways into her face and pulled her collar closer. The wind was still picking up. The buff-colored fragmite was flattened out like wheat before the scythe. He could see whitecaps just beyond the dock, frothy clumps that bunched and flexed with the gusts.

"Bailey?"

"Oh God," he breathed, almost to himself. "Why would he take her out in this, and alone? Where would he go? How far?"

Sis watched, waiting for him to finish his thought, but Bailey stopped and swallowed. Maybe he's just out of sight and sound, a little way upriver in the bight. Turning into the northeast wind as he pulled away from the dock could have been tricky, but it would be safer than trying to go farther downriver.

Heart hammering, Bailey made his way back out to the end of the dock, into the teeth of the wind, his resentment at Booty's claiming the boat dissolving in a rising tide of fear.

He can't be too far, he thought. *And he's got the radio. He'd radio if he was in trouble.*

But as his mind raced, Bailey began to wonder. With every other waterman safely at home, who would Booty radio? And if he did, how far would the signal carry in this weather? Bounce was a funny thing. Sometimes you could talk with watermen as far down as Bloody Point. Other times, you were lucky to reach someone a half a mile away.

At the end of the dock he stood, craned forward, listening, hoping. *When did he leave? Maybe he's only just gone out and seen it's too bad and will be right back*, he said to himself. *Maybe he just needed to prove to me he could get out there before me. Maybe he needed* . . .

He stopped, unwilling to speculate. He pulled off his hat and tilted his head around at a different angle to the wind until he could hear the sleet singing into the water, hoping for the sound of an engine. Bits of ice pelted his ear; he cupped his hand around it the way the old watermen, deafened by years of standing by a roaring engine, did to hear normal conversation. He felt Sis, who had crabbed her way out to him at the end of the dock, grab his arm.

"Bailey!" she screamed. "We gotta get Tud!"

Bailey looked at her, considering. Tud. Holed up in his warm living room, maybe already nipping at a bottle, feeling sorry for himself. What would—or could—Tud do? Besides, Booty could be just around a bend, perfectly safe, tonging oysters to bring home for Thanksgiving. Bailey tried to summon anger. He told himself he'd been betrayed, that Booty deserved whatever battle he was fighting out there. Feeling angry helped stave off the fear—and guilt.

"Come on!" Sis urged, steadying herself in a half crouch. "Let's go!"

He wanted to stay there and wait for Booty to come back in, then to let him have it. *Booty'll be back in*, he assured himself, pushing away doubt. *Running around raising alarms will just make me look foolish*. But Sis refused to let him go. She had taken a step backwards, still gripping his sleeve. Bailey turned to snarl at her, but at the sight of her face, eyes wide and cheeks ashen, his own fear welled up again, thudded in his ears, pounded against his chest. He tried to shove it away, but it came on him now in a wave, crashing over him, draining away his confidence.

"Come on, Bailey," Sis urged again. "We gotta get Tud."

Bailey squinted into the storm, hoping—praying—to see a ghostly form emerge headed back toward them. Nothing.

"Bailey!"

He nodded and let her lead him, grabbing her when she stumbled. They climbed back into their truck. Bailey started it, shifted it into gear, and eased it into a turn. The truck skated a little on the slick roadway, thumping against the side of Tud's truck and shoving it further into the ditch. Backing up, he managed to negotiate a sloppy three-point turn and head back up the road. The sleet had begun to penetrate the arced trees now, coating the macadam with ice. At the road's end, he pumped the brakes to stop, but the truck only slowed; they slid through the stop sign and out into Bourneville Road, skidding across first one then the other lane toward the ditch on the other side.

Sis let out a yelp, then bit her lip and clutched the seat in silence. Turning the wheel slowly, Bailey brought the truck's nose around until they straddled the yellow double line. No one was on the road. They crept into town at twenty miles an hour, hardly daring to breathe, and turned into Hanson's empty parking lot.

"I'll call Tud," Bailey said, opening the door.

"What'll you say to him?" Sis cried, but Bailey slammed the door on her words.

The restaurant was locked. He skittered along the boardwalk to the pay phone outside, picked up the receiver, shoved change into the slot, and dialed. He counted seven rings before Tud picked up.

"Yeah?"

Tud's voice sounded thick.

"It's Bailey."

"Yeah?"

"Booty took *Leah Jean* out," Bailey said.

"Huh?"

"I said, Booty's got *Leah Jean* out in this. I think he's alone."

"Out in what?"

"Haven't you looked outside yet?" Bailey demanded, voice rising.

He heard Tud put down the phone and lumber to the window, then heard his clambering run as he snatched up the phone again.

"God!" Tud moaned. "Oh God! Out in this? Are you sure?"

"*Leah Jean*'s gone."

"Damn fool," Tud swore. "You know where he went?"

"I was hopin' you'd know. He wouldn't have gone outside the bight, you think?"

"How should I know what he's done?" Tud cried. "What the hell's he doin' going' out alone in this? You s'posed to be together today, weren't you?"

Bailey didn't answer.

"God," Tud said again.

"Whadda we do?"

"I'll call Wiley and Bill and the Boss twins and Iggie Driscoll," Tud said, ticking off long-time competitors. "Their wives can call a few more. I'm gonna kill that boy when we find him. You call Uncle Buddy and Jim Nagle."

"I don't have any more money."

"Where the hell are you?"

"Hanson's. No one's around."

"Call Emma and tell her. Operator'll let you phone home."

Tud hung up, and Bailey put his finger on the cradle for a new dial tone, his teeth chattering. He was grateful to hear Tud's automatic threat to kill Booty when he got hold of him, a talisman against unthinkable possibilities. It made things seem almost normal. The operator eventually connected him to home. The phone only rang once before Emma picked it up.

"Where on earth are you?" she demanded. "I was worried sick when I got up and found you both gone. I could smack you so hard—"

"Booty's out on *Leah Jean* alone," Bailey interrupted.

"Dear Lord."

Bailey could hear her breath quicken, urging his own heart faster.

"I called Tud. He's callin' some of the others. He wants you to call Jim Nagle and Uncle Buddy."

"Okay."

"And anybody else you can think of."

"Yeah. What about Sis?"

"She's with me."

"I don't want you going out with them."

"Mom . . ."

There was a pause and then Emma said, "All right. But don't take Sis. I'm comin' down as soon as I phone."

"Mom? Get Tud as soon's you can. Booty took his truck."

"I'll get him."

She hung up and Bailey stood there a moment, shaking, trying to bring back the sound of Tud's voice when he said he'd kill Booty, the implied certainty of his safe return. The wind blasted through the standing rigging of the few sailboats docked at the piers for the winter, their halyards beating a frantic tattoo against aluminum masts. Sis sat in the truck, her eyes on Bailey. She looked bleary through the windshield, though the windshield wipers were still going. He stumbled back, climbed into the cab, and slammed the door. He had left the engine running and the interior was warm, but he couldn't stop shaking. He felt helpless just sitting there. Gusts blasted across the river and rocked the truck. Fifty knots now, he guessed. Maybe sixty. *God, Booty. Where are you?*

Maybe he's back, he thought. *Maybe we should go back down to Otto's to see if he's back.*

He reached for the gearshift.

"What are you doin'?" Sis demanded.

"I'm goin' back down to see if he's come in."

"Stay," Sis said emphatically.

"He could be back in by now. And Tud locks his boat up so I can't get her ready," Bailey said. "He probably won't want me aboard anyway. He and Mom'll have a whole posse down in a little while. I'll feel like a idiot if they all get down here and Booty's already in."

Bailey locked eyes with her for a moment.

"Stay here," she commanded.

Bailey was too scared to bristle. He studied her for a moment, the warring terror and determination in her eyes. But her voice was firm. Firm enough that he trusted the instinct behind it. Dropping his hands, he turned to watch the storm slice across the river, stomach churning.

"What're you gonna do?" Sis asked finally.

"Pray we find him," Bailey replied.

fourteen

T hey sat in silence while the sleet pinged against the metal truck, drumming on the hood in erratic time with the gusts. Finally, a pickup turned into the parking lot—the Boss twins—followed by Iggie Driscoll, then Emma's station wagon, then two more trucks. Like a circus act, they skidded to a stop, side by side in the shelter of the restaurant. Doors flew open and several men, massive, armored in yellow foul-weather gear and gloves, climbed out, their faces stony. Emma, bareheaded and gloveless, made her way around to where Tud now stood with the men who had clumped together at the corner of the restaurant. She caught Tud by the sleeve.

"You'll find him," she said.

Tud looked at her blankly, then turned his attention back to Iggie.

"All right, boys," Iggie said, his voice hard, "let's get out there and run down in a line. We keep in sight of each other. Keep your eyes peeled for anything."

All unconsciously bowed their heads as each man tried not to imagine what they might find—a pair of tongs bobbing with their tips just visible, a seat cushion, the boat itself, filled to the gunwales, only its canopy and blank-eyed windows visible above the surface.

"He's probably just ducked behind Cathers Bight," Iggie said, pumping hope back into the search party, "He'll be tucked up snug, tongin' away, mad we've broke in on his private time. He'll have a good laugh at all of us comin' down on 'im like the damn cavalry!"

He forced a grin and heard answering grunts from the others, a prayer of sorts, offered and confirmed. Bailey had slogged over to stand at the edge of the group, looking from one seamed face to the next, hoping someone—anyone but Tud—would take him. Heavy with dread, he waited.

"Come on, Bailey!" Tud growled. "You're comin' with me!"

Bailey swallowed and darted desperate looks around the circle of men, but none met his gaze. Turning, they headed for the boats, some of them hobbling on joints stiff from years of injury and cold. Two more trucks pulled up. Four more slicker-clad watermen climbed out and set off down the dock behind the others.

Emma stood and watched them go, immune to the sleet that plastered her hair to her head. Crossing the parking lot, she pulled open the truck door and climbed in next to her daughter.

"Will they find him?" Sis asked in a small voice.

"Yeah," Emma nodded, watching the men go down the dock, Bailey trailing Tud. "They'll find him."

She reached toward Sis but withdrew her hand when she saw the girl stiffen, unwilling to be comforted.

"They've got to find him," Sis said indignantly. "That's all there is to it. They've just got to find him."

Emma studied Sis. The loss of Orrin—alive at breakfast one morning and gone before supper that night—was a hard, hard lesson on the fragility of life. Booty's got to come home, Emma agreed silently. That's all there is to it.

"Come here, Sissypants," she said gently, reaching again toward her daughter. This time, Sis relented and crawled across the seat to curl into her mother's arms.

"CHANNEL SIXTEEN," Iggie yelled from his cockpit, raising his hand-held radio toward the others who were climbing aboard boats.

"Roger that, sixteen," a couple of men acknowledged with their heads down, eyes on their precarious footing. "And no one leaves sight of the next," Iggie continued, his voice hoarse against the wind. "We go down in a line like the Mummers' parade!"

Nods of understanding and agreement this time, a hand up, a brief wave, but no words. Tud climbed aboard *Evelyn Louise*, unlocked the cabin, then cranked up the old engine. Miraculously, it roared to life.

"Cast off!" he shouted.

Bailey flung the lines off one by one, the usually graceful arc of his cast crumpled by the wind. He came carefully along the slick deck and stepped down onto the cockpit floor.

"Get the radio," Tud barked. "Stand by."

Obediently, Bailey went forward and reached into the cabin to snatch the hand radio from its charger, which was screwed to the bulkhead. He turned it on and fiddled with the knob until he caught the tail end of a radio check between Rufus Boss and Wiley Johns.

One by one the low-slung boats—some open to the elements, others with canopies that acted as a shield if not a shelter—moved out of their slips and hovered like gulls in the channel, engines working against the wind, waiting for the flotilla to mass. There was safety in numbers. Keeping his ear by the radio, Bailey thought again of Booty alone and tried to imagine him as Iggie had described, tucked up in Cathers Bight out of sight just northeast—windward—of Otto's dock, protected by Deep Point, tonging happily. *If he's done that, and kept* Leah Jean *idling ahead into the wind, he'll be okay*, Bailey thought. The biggest problem would be to turn her to go back to the dock. *Leah Jean* would ride a swell with grace and confidence— if Booty kept her from running broadside to the waves.

"Pay attention!" Tud shouted. "Keep a lookout on the port side."

Silently, Bailey complied, pulling his collar up against the sleet that ran down his neck. Huddled beneath the overhang that jutted off the cabin roof, he saw the boats fan out, their captains gauging their speed so no one would be left behind.

They ran along in phalanx, the outermost vessels sometimes sliding into the channel to avoid a shoal, at other times stretching the line out nearly to the riverbanks. They were running half-blind, the horizon obliterated. Buoys, reeling like punch-drunk fighters before the wind's pummeling hand, loomed up then fell quickly behind, swallowed again.

Bailey, not daring to speak, was alone with his thoughts. He scanned the space ahead, hoping to see the familiar line of *Leah Jean*'s bow, the swoop of her decks, with Booty standing in her cockpit, tonging. Nothing. *We couldn't hear him if he shouted*, Bailey thought. He cast a look astern in case they had bypassed any small piece of evidence, some marker that would point toward Booty. Unwillingly, his glance fell on Tud, who stood unprotected, one rubber-gloved hand on the tiller, the other gripping the upright he had nailed to the engine cover for balance in rough seas, his face a mask, the eyes dark, unreadable slits.

Tud had been angry as long as Bailey could remember, snarling at friends and strangers alike, in perpetual war against the world. Some of his worst barbs were directed at Booty, an inexplicable cruelty. Orrin had once said that if you hadn't known Tud before Lottie left, you couldn't really know Tud. Until this moment, Bailey had seen Tud's harsh words as meanness. But seeing Tud bent against the gale as he drove forward, jaw clenched, Bailey saw that his anger was not meanness but pain, the howl of a broken soul. Tud looked at Bailey. Bailey wanted to offer some encouragement, or to be given some, but Tud turned away again.

Iggie's voice squawked over the radio.

"Anybody see anything yet?"

It was a rhetorical question, meant to connect rather than communicate. They all knew that the minute anyone saw anything, no matter how small, they'd be on the radio, hollering.

"Nope, naw, nothin'," voices responded.

"We thought we mighta seed somethin', but it was a storage box blowed off somebody's bulkhead," Wiley Johns added to keep up the conversation. "Where would he of gone, Bailey?"

Where could he have gone? Bailey wondered desperately.

"I don't know," Bailey replied. "We bin keepin' the boat down by Telfordtown, so we could get in an' out quicker." He paused, feeling as if he were saying too much. "I bin tryin' to think like him. . . ." He faltered again, glancing at Tud who could see him talking but could not make out the words over the wind.

"What're they sayin'?" Tud demanded.

"They want to know where he woulda gone," Bailey shouted back. "Do you . . ." He hesitated, unsure whether or not even to ask, whether the question would imply some criticism of their relationship, their knowledge of each other, then went on. "Do you and him have any favorite places for foul weather he'da tried?"

"Naw, naw," Tud said shaking his head. "Favorite places. Naw. I can't think o' none," he went on, eyes smoldering. "We never went out in stink like this. Krafts're the only ones stupid enough to go out in this."

It was an accusation, bait for a fight. But Bailey held his tongue. Too much was at stake for distractions.

"Tud doesn't know of any place either," Bailey said into the radio.

"Roger that," Iggie replied. "Roger that. We'll fan out into the bight when we get there."

He didn't say that if they still hadn't found Booty by the time they reached the place where the river widens, where the wind would be howling across the shoals out of the broad Eastern Branch, building deep, breaking waves that could capsize them regardless of their numbers, they'd have another decision to make—whether to keep going or turn back, to save their own boats and lives.

At Cathers Bight, Tud ducked out of line and slid behind the point into the scooped-out basin. He cut along the edge of the deeper water, eyes darting, unconsciously chewing his lip. Bailey scanned across both sides of the boat, squinting at every darkened splotch, every light edge that might have been a part of the *Leah Jean*, praying that when they got to Otto's dock they would find the boat safely moored, straining at her doubled-up lines, and Booty struggling to get Tud's truck out of the ditch.

They worked their way around the west shore, past the dock at Telfordtown. Bailey held his breath, willing *Leah Jean* to materialize out of the gray. The muscles in his neck, tense from craning forward, ached. As the dim outline of Otto's dock came into view, his heart leaped. A darker line swept along its edge—the boat? Bailey stood up on his toes to peer over the cabin roof. He could see a shape, barely distinguishable but darker than the pier. *Let it be the* Leah Jean, he prayed. They bore down on it, but as they approached he realized the dark line had been a wave, already rolling past the dock to crash against the ice-covered beach. The dock was empty. Where was Booty? *Please, Dad, help us, do it now. What do we do?* Ghosts welled up, memories of Krafts, but they were mocking, beyond his reach. He felt utterly alone.

"Thought he might a' been back," Tud shouted, jerking his head toward the empty dock.

Bailey nodded.

"Okay," Iggie said. "Let's keep going, boys. Have a care as we cross Eastern Branch. Stay in sight."

So Iggie had made the decision. Keep going. At least a little further. Though the transmission was inaudible to him, Tud urged *Evelyn Louise* back into her place in the phalanx, shoulders bowed, determined to plow on no matter what the others decided. As they approached the joint of the upper Elizabeth, the Eastern Branch, and Fulton Bay, they slowed, taking the measure of the waves.

"Let's fan out more," Iggie shouted over the radio, a current of rising tension in his voice. "Careful to keep the seas on your aft quarter, and for God's sake, don't run aground!"

As they left the protection of Rebels Neck, they could just make out the big red nun that marked the channel laid out before the wind like a gaudy corpse. As the river widened, they stretched the distance between the boats, edging out to the limits of their sight. It wasn't enough. The river was three miles wide. Together, they could only cover a half a mile at a time.

"Everybody okay?" Iggie radioed down the line.

A series of acknowledgments came back in reply.

"Keep a sharp eye out," he urged unnecessarily, "and everybody keep in touch."

"Whoa!" Wiley's voice came over the radio. "Who put that shoal there?" he laughed, but it was bravado, not amusement. Running aground now could mean capsizing, or sinking, as the boat pounded up and down against the river bottom, working her seams open or staving in her hull. A potential death sentence in a winter storm.

"You okay, Wiley?" Iggie radioed back.

"Yeah. She's a-rockin' an' a-rollin', but so far so good."

"How's everybody else holdin' up?"

Bailey looked at Tud. He had shrunk into himself, lips compressed into a thin line, face washed in rivulets of icy water. But his eyes, blue-black slits, moved continuously, like a hungry animal's desperate for his prey.

"Tud and me're okay," Bailey radioed.

It was a lie. The longer they went without seeing *Leah Jean*, the less okay they were.

"We're startin' to get slapped around some," Rob Boss said.

"How's yer ice?" Iggie asked.

The spray and sleet, freezing as it hit the decks, was coating the boats, layer upon heavy layer that changed their motion from a predictable side-to-side slosh to a sickeningly sluggish roll. More than one fishing boat had gone down when a wave, breaking onto an ice-heavy stern, swamped it. Bailey remembered the family who had lost three sons to a single, final wave that had washed into their thickly coated cockpit already loaded down with fish. Only one mile from shore, with a full catch on board that would have paid off the boat loan, they were gone. They never had a chance.

"Not great," Rob replied.

"What do ya think, Bailey? Could he be in Fulton Creek?"

Bailey thought a moment and cast a hopeful look up the creek, a nasty westerly turn broadside to the rollers, but a protected harbor once they were inside.

"Maybe," he said. "He might."

"What?" Tud asked, seeing the hope on Bailey's face.

"Fulton!" Bailey shouted to him. "He mighta gone into Fulton."

Tud lifted his head a little.

"Yeah. He might at that."

He started to make the turn around Nichols Point, cutting across the shoal that jutted half a mile out into the river.

"Wait!" Bailey cried. "It's too soon!"

"Don't you give me orders, boy!" Tud snapped. "I bin runnin' this river long before you was even a twinkle in yer daddy's eye."

"Iggie!" Bailey radioed. "Tud's makin' the turn now."

"Tell him to wait another ten minutes," Iggie said.

"Iggie says to wait ten minutes more 'til he says to go, and everyone'll turn at the same time," Bailey relayed to Tud, adding the explanation he assumed Iggie hadn't bothered to make, the one that he hoped would persuade Tud.

Tud glared at Bailey, his body a column of resistance, but he swung *Evelyn Louise*'s stern back across the waves to set a course parallel to the others. A wave rolled over the transom and broke into the cockpit, running down into the bilge between hull and floorboards.

"Get the pump goin'!" Tud shouted, pointing to the rusted instrument panel on the bulkhead beside the radio charger.

Bailey leaned in and flipped the switch on.

"Is it going?" He shouted back to Tud.

Tud put his head down against the engine casing, listened a moment, then gave Bailey a thumbs up. Bailey nodded and returned his attention to the river. Row on row of breakers boiled out of the Eastern Branch and rolled into the bleak distance across the long open span to Torys Prize. He shivered involuntarily and braced himself against the coaming. His feet and bare hands ached with cold. His gloves were on *Leah Jean*. He stuck the radio under his arm and tucked his hands under his jacket. His hat was soaked and felt frozen to his skull. Hypothermia. He tried to comfort himself with the memory of Ludlow Kraft dragging the capsized log canoe ashore and retonging all the oysters he had lost, nearly freezing to death in the process. It didn't help. He now wondered if the story were even true. If any of the Kraft stories were true.

"All right, boys, let's make it a pretty turn now," Iggie said, his voice muffled against Bailey's foul-weather gear. "Just like the Blue Angels."

Bailey almost smiled at Iggie's comparison with the Navy's exhibition team of fighter jets. The Angels' precision movements, executed within yards of each other at 150 miles per hour a thousand feet in the air, replicated this miserable slog in a sixty-knot gale in only one way: one false move meant disaster. Bailey had admired the Blue Angels from the time he had first seen them, their skill, the daring of their aerobatic choreography, their courage. Looking across the dark water at the Boss twins, visible in ephemeral outline through the sleet, Bailey realized that this was courage, too, and something more. Generosity. There was no glamour, no admiring audience. They could have been safely at home, warm, anticipating a Thanksgiving feast—simple well-earned pleasures. Tud had even made enemies of some of these men. Yet they were here. Shepherds all seeking one lost sheep.

The turn would be hardest for Bill Bligh in *Boopsie*, farthest upwind and without the small protection of other hulls to mitigate the worst of the wind and waves. Tud had begun the turn, his full attention on the mouth of Fulton, where he hoped to find his son.

"*Boopsie*? How're you doin'?" Iggie's worry crackled through the line.

"So far so good," Bill came back.

"Keep in close touch," Iggie commanded. "How's everybody else?"

"Still here," Rob Boss gasped.

"Took a sea over the stern, but the pump's stayin' ahead of it," Jim Nagle informed them all.

"Scuddy?"

Bailey listened, waiting for Scuddy Bleak to report.

"*Lorna*?" Iggie said again, calling him this time by boat name.

"Yeah! We're here," Scuddy replied finally, sending a collective sigh through the fleet. "For a sec I thought we'd done, but we're around."

"Everybody else around?"

"Yeah. We're fine. Yeah, we made it," came the replies.

"That'll be the worst of it," Iggie assured them, affirming aloud what all knew from long experience. "Let those suckers chase us on into the creek."

They rode for ten minutes without contact, yawing across the following seas, working hard to keep from broaching without putting too much strain on the steering.

"I'm in!" Rob Boss cried finally. "Blessed peace!"

"You see anything?" Bailey demanded over the radio.

"Nope. Not yet."

"What?" Tud asked.

"Rob and Rufus are inside Fulton," Bailey explained. "But they don't see anything yet."

Tud nodded, his expression blank though every fiber of his body bent toward the creek.

136

"I'm around!" Jim Nagle called over the radio.

"Got anything yet, Jim?" Iggie asked.

"Nope. Just a whole load o' nothin'."

fifteen

O ne by one they crossed the channel and slid under the lee of the point. The line between the breakers that rolled across the mouth and the lower waves that corrugated Fulton Creek was as straight and clear as though drawn with a ruler. As, one by one, they crossed that line into calmer water, they closed the gaps between them, running northwest up into the interior, careful to avoid the sandy shelf of shallow water on either side of the entrance.

"How're we doin'?" Iggie called out.

"Okay, okay," the replies came back with weary resignation.

The tension of keeping themselves and their own boats intact and the knowledge that the longer they looked for Booty, the less likely they were to find him, weighed on all of them.

"He could be way up there! We need to run the whole thing," Tud shouted, daring Bailey to disagree.

Bailey nodded and relayed the message to Iggie.

"Roger that," Iggie came back. "We'll check all the coves."

Deep Cove, facetiously named since only canoes and waders could navigate its puddle-like depths, was out, though Bill Bligh ran as close as he dared while peering into it through binoculars.

"Not in Deep Cove," he reported as they passed.

"Roger."

"I'll run into Long Cove," Iggie volunteered. "I go in pretty regular." Slowing, he ducked behind the line of boats and puttered into the little harbor. In a few minutes, he came back out again. "Nothin'."

"He wouldn'ta gone into Lawyers Cove," Rob Boss observed.

No one could get in there. Shallow and wreck-strewn, Lawyers Cove was just as they all envisioned the law—a series of uncharted obstacles set to snare the unwary.

"Maybe he's holed up at Billard's," Scuddy said, his gravelly voice mixing with the grating reception on the radio.

"Maybe he's at Billard's," Tud said, breaking his silence.

Bailey nodded and held the radio up.

"That's what Scuddy just said, too." Bailey almost added, *Maybe that's a good sign*, then stopped. Better to rejoice when they finally found him, he decided, not look for signs and wonders.

Tud was wearing down, Bailey could tell. He looked as though he had a stone lashed to his neck that was slowly bending him in half, dragging his chin toward the floorboards.

"Check that bilge pump!" he barked at Bailey.

Bailey nodded. He lifted the engine cover up and peered down into the dark, oily bilge. The pump was sucking up the last of the wave they had taken aboard. A cloying smell of burning rubber rose from the hole. Bailey went to the instrument panel and shut it off.

"When's the last time you had that pump apart?" he asked, without thinking. It was an automatic question, an implied criticism. The minute it was out of his mouth, he could have bitten his tongue in half.

Tud glared at him.

"Don't give me none o' that Kraft 'I'm better'n you' crap!" he snarled. "Yer daddy'd be alive today if he didn't have to be so damned perfect all the time, keepin' it all in. It's wearin' on a man to have to be better'n everybody."

"Shut up!" Bailey exploded. "What would you know about it? He was a better waterman than you'll ever be if you live to be a hundred!"

"You come across here and say that, you little pissant!" Tud yelled, making a fist with his free hand.

140

"He ain't at Billard's," Scuddy's voice sounded over the radio, slicing through the tension between Bailey and Tud.

"Right," Iggie replied, the discouragement evident even through the faulty reception. "Let's split in half at Cacaway and sweep the rest of the creek. Stay in touch."

As they approached Cacaway Island, the flotilla divided. Tud and Bailey slid into the protected East Fork with Rob and Rufus Boss on *Jeabo*. In there, running between the tree-lined shores, the storm seemed contained, manageable. Wind and sleet pelted them on the starboard side, and Bailey pulled his collar up farther to keep the icy water from running down his neck. The houses and docks were almost visible in gray outline, even from the center of the narrow creek, and the chop was short, barely whitecapped.

"Gimme that radio," Tud demanded, sticking his hand out, waiting.

Bailey hesitated, stung by Tud's angry accusation about his family—about his father. Worse, a small voice at the back of his head whispered that there might be truth in it. For a second, he wanted to exact some small revenge. But Tud's hand, thick as a slab of steak, reached toward him, unwavering. Finally, Bailey leaned out and handed over the radio.

"You see anything over there, Rob?" Tud called into the mouthpiece, holding it so close he looked as though he were chewing on it.

"Not yet," came the reply.

Tud noted the optimistic *yet*, but Rob Boss's tone betrayed lost hope.

"Damn!" Tud growled.

Though Bailey couldn't hear the exchange he could guess it accurately enough. He sat on the port rail, scanning the ice-coated banks desultorily as they churned up into the narrowing branch. It took fifteen minutes to reach the head of the creek at Flat Point. As they turned around, their props stirring up the muddy bottom, Bailey could feel his chest tighten. *That's it*, he thought. *He's out there somewhere in that mess.*

He had no business takin' Leah Jean *out when I told him not to. This ain't my fault.*

He tried to comfort himself with this absolution, but it was futile. He felt responsible. There had been an unspoken challenge between them ever since the day Booty had set foot on *Leah Jean*, one that Booty couldn't afford to lose—and Bailey knew it. He had goaded Booty, dared him to want more than he had. The day Bailey had fallen over—a shameful sloppiness on his part—Booty had jumped in after him by instinct, even though it was against all common wisdom. It was an act of unwavering friendship. And Bailey had flung it back in his face.

Tud cradled the radio against his chest, squinting into the murky distance as they turned back toward Cacaway and a rendezvous with the other members of their search party. Now they would make a decision about whether or not to go on. Regardless of what anyone else determined, Bailey knew what he had to do.

The deck was barely visible through building layers of ice that thickened the boat's contours, weighing her down. She moved drunkenly, answering the helm with out-sized swings. Bailey wondered how she'd be out in the sideways seas of the broad Elizabeth River. Eastern Neck. Booty might have run all the way down and made it around the end, then couldn't get back. He could be there, running out his fuel. The possibility was hopeful but also presented a new panic, a new deadline. If Booty were there, he'd need help soon—unless he could run her up on shore and climb off. Bailey wondered if he'd abandon the boat he was working so hard to own, the boat that wasn't even half his yet was his whole hope.

He looked at Tud. The grizzled jaw was clenched so hard it was white. Melted sleet dripped off his chin and down into his shirt. There was no question what Tud would do. The only question was, *Will anybody else go with us?*

As they edged out from behind Cacaway he could see the prows emerging from the West Fork into Fulton Creek.

"Anything?" Tud asked over the radio without bothering to call a name. The question was unnecessary. He knew that even a false sighting would have brought a whoop.

"Nope."

It was Iggie. His voice sounded final.

"Let's head on out along Torys Prize . . ." Tud began.

Bailey watched Tud but was unable to hear his words.

"Tud—," Iggie said, but Tud mashed his thumb against the TALK button on the radio and cut him off.

"I say we go and look along Eastern Neck," Tud repeated. "He coulda snuck down there earlier and be holed up on the leeward side, maybe even runnin' out o' fuel, hopin' for a tow."

"Tud," Iggie began again. "I ain't goin'. I got a family. If he's out there, he's gonna hafta drop a hook and hang on. Booty's got sense."

Bailey saw a look of desperation cross Tud's face.

"If he had sense he wouldn't be out in this crap!" Tud cried, his voice breaking.

"I'd do it for your son, you know I would," he persisted, pleading with Iggie to keep the search party going.

"We all got families," Iggie repeated doggedly. He was speaking not only for himself but also for the anxious watermen on the other boats and for their wives and children at home, praying—both for Booty and for the safe return of their men. "If he's around the back side of Eastern Neck, he'll stay there. Maybe he got 'round before it kicked up too bad. We're gonna lose somebody going out there in this now."

There was silence. No dissenting voices. Iggie had spoken everyone's thought. The decision had been made.

"You bastards!" Tud screamed into the radio. "I'll do it alone. I'da done it for any one o' you, but you just go home and eat your turkey dinners. I'll find him by myself."

Iggie didn't bother to respond to Tud's insult. He didn't say, "We're all out here. Searching. Risking our lives on Thanksgiving Day. But there's a limit." He understood Tud's desperation even while he hated Tud's ingratitude for what they had all done already. When was enough enough? When someone went down looking? He sighed, shooting a glance across their tenuously linked line of bateaux, huddled close enough in the basin so they could see each other: the Boss twins in *Jeabo*; Uncle Buddy, his massive bulk wrapped around the strut that held up his cabin top, in *Jemima*; the others hunched against the wind and sleet, throttled back, waiting.

"We done all we could for now," Iggie said, his voice hard, practical.

"We ain't done all we could 'til we go out around Eastern Neck," Tud insisted.

"What about Bailey?" Iggie asked. "Don't he get a choice?"

Tud glared at Bailey, who was hunched, back to the howling wind, against the slippery rail.

"He stays with me," Tud replied, not bothering to ask Bailey.

Bailey looked at Tud, saw the new, wild-eyed anger, the half-crazed determination. His throat constricted. He's gonna kill us both, he thought.

"I'm gonna tie up at Billard's," Iggie said, "and call Doris."

Tud looked up to see two of the boats already heading for the protection of the marina.

"Come with us, Tud. We done all we can do."

"We ain't done all we can do!" Tud screamed into the radio again. "I'm goin' back out there and find him."

"Tud . . . ," Iggie said, then stopped. "Good luck."

"Shit!" Tud threw the radio down onto the engine box. It skidded off to land by Bailey's half-frozen feet. Bailey picked it up and turned a knob.

"You still read me?" he asked Iggie.

"That you, Bailey?"

"Yeah."

"He's goin' back out, boy. You don't hafta go with him. Your mama needs you now. She couldn't take it if she lost you, too. Let me come pick you up and take you into Billard's with us."

Bailey shook his head, his eyes locked on Iggie's across the water.

"No. I better stay."

"You don't hafta do this, Bailey," Iggie repeated firmly. "We done all we could. You didn't send him out in this. No sense in your losing your life tryin' to find him. Think o' your mama. If Booty's okay, he's okay. He's anchored and ridin' it out. If he ain't okay, our bein' out there ain't gonna make any more difference to him."

Iggie's words, the first acknowledgment that Booty could be gone, clawed at Bailey's gut. He felt as though the deck were falling away from him for a second. *If he ain't okay . . .*

"I gotta go," Bailey said, pushing away the fear.

"I think you're makin' a big mistake," Iggie said. Then added, "We'll keep our radios on."

Tud and Bailey headed back down Fulton Bay. The others peeled off and scooted for the half-empty piers of Billard's Marina, where the few boats still in the water thrashed against their dock lines like anxious horses.

Bailey felt suffocated with loneliness. They were on their own. He looked at Tud, a column of will bent toward the river and Booty. The waves grew sharper and deeper as they ground on toward the mouth of Fulton Bay.

As the waves grew, so did Bailey's fear. He tried to draw into his mind a picture of one of those airless late-summer days when the water undulated like molten gunmetal and the world seemed to hold its breath. He couldn't. This churning body was unrecognizable as the river he knew so well. Everything was chaos with nothing to cling to but this small, unstable boat. Squinting, Bailey could just make out the shadowy outline of Nicholas Point and beyond that, the breakers galloping across the mouth of Fulton. Clamping his mouth shut against the scream of protest he wanted to raise, he held on as they lurched out into the storm.

They turned south again, heading for Torys Prize. As they passed the can off Windmill Point, a wave slapped them broadside, lifting the stern and threatening to bury the bow. Bailey hunkered down, praying to a God he wasn't sure he believed in, and waited. He heard a frantic roar as the engine came up out of the water entirely, its propeller beating the air and threatening to overrun its governor. She lurched, nose into the trough. Bailey crashed to the deck, landing on his knees, clawing for a handhold. Just as he feared she'd submarine nose first, *Evelyn Louise*'s stern slapped back down into the trough, submerging the prop. He fell back against the bulkhead. Tud slumped over the coaming, head and shoulders in the water, legs splayed out behind him in a reluctant dive.

"No!" Bailey screamed.

He skittered over to Tud, terrified that his added weight would be just enough to capsize the already beleaguered boat. But as she lifted her bow out of the wave, *Evelyn Louise* leaned back on her heels. It was just enough. Bailey caught Tud by the top of his foul-weather gear and dragged him back aboard. Choking, his face gray, Tud wrapped one arm around the strut and fumbled for the tiller.

"You all right?" Bailey shouted.

Tud nodded, coughing, and waved Bailey back across to the port side. Another wave dropped the boat into a trough. Bailey looked up to see nothing but white water, a wall suspended above his head.

This is it, he thought, and slithered beneath the narrow shelter of the side as the wave crashed onto the deck, washing down into the cabin and along the gaps in the engine box to the bilge.

"Get that pump goin' again!" Tud shouted, as the green can off Cardiff Creek Point whisked by their starboard side.

Bailey struggled to the cabin and flicked on the bilge pump again. As he looked up, he saw the green can sweep across their stern, heading east, the wrong direction, evidence of a dangerous slide toward shore.

"Keep her off the shore!" Bailey shouted, pointing toward the swiftly receding buoy.

Ignoring Bailey, Tud urged the boat along the shallow ledge at Piney Neck. Bailey felt a lurch.

"We've hit, Tud!" he screamed. "Port rudder! We're too close in. Get us off the beach or we're gonna get beat to pieces!"

Tud darted a murderous look in his direction but shoved the tiller over. The boat refused to answer the helm. She was getting pushed farther and farther into shore. Tud swore, leaning harder against the tiller until Bailey was afraid it would break. Finally, the bow bounced around toward the east into the pounding waves until they were nearly broadside to the wind. Bailey watched the waves boil and tumble toward them, grabbing for their boat. Every second or third one poured over the coaming and into the bilge. The pump couldn't keep up. Bailey grabbed a bucket and wrapped one leg around the strut. Blood pumping, arms and legs aching, he frantically pushed water back over the side, but *Evelyn Louise* was slowly filling up. She moved sluggishly, as though giving up, just waiting for the river to claim her.

"No!" Bailey screamed. She couldn't give in. *Once your boat gives up, ain't nothin' you can do.* He'd heard it often enough and knew it must be true. *Evelyn Louise* had to keep fighting with them if they were to survive.

Soaked through, fingers burning with cold, he could feel the sweat trickle down his neck beneath his foul-weather gear. His left foot slipped and the leg shot out, yanking his hip painfully, but he had automatically tightened up on the strut with his right leg, holding himself up like a trapeze artist clinging to a single wooden bar. He scooped and flung water out of the boat and back into the river until he thought his back would break. Then, he noticed the angle of the waves changing. Fewer were coming in over the coaming. Lifting his head, he could just make out the dim outline of Cardiff Creek Point working along the starboard side.

We're going into Cardiff Creek, he thought with a flood of relief. *We're going to live.* Bailey had almost forgotten why they were out there, what was driving Tud forward. He was focused only on his own survival. He redoubled his efforts at bailing, certain now they would make it.

BOOM! The boat hit hard. Bailey lost his footing completely and crashed against the engine box, then sprawled on the deck. A rivulet of warmth oozed down his face, an odd feeling where it mingled with the icy sleet. Diluted blood splashed onto the deck. Tud had turned too soon.

"Tud! Hard port! Hard port!" Bailey screamed, clawing himself upright to see a jagged piling, all that was left of an old dock, rise out of the water just off the starboard side.

Tud was already struggling to bring the boat around into deeper water, but she was being swept further and further onto the shoals. The stern lifted up again, and the propeller, absent the water's resistance, protested in a high-pitched whine. *Evelyn Louise* hesitated, then came down again—BAM!—sending a sickening shiver through her hull. The waves kept coming, an inexhaustible army set against them. She rose again, then smashed down—BAM!—old planking crushed onto the debris-strewn shoal.

"She's gonna break up!" Bailey cried.

"The hell she is!" Tud roared. He leaned into the strut, connecting his body with the boat, willing *Evelyn Louise* forward as he shoved the tiller hard over. "Come on, you bitch, get offa here!"

BAM! She came down again. Bailey's heart thudded hard in his chest.

"Come on, come on!" Tud demanded.

The boat heeled into the wind, her starboard quarter caught up against a lump. A freezing wave poured in and sloshed around their ankles.

"Bail!" Tud ordered.

Bailey grabbed the bucket and heaved icy water over the side. He could barely feel his fingers. They lurched off, then grounded, and he fell to his knees, but he kept bailing, buoyed by Tud's determination. *Evelyn Louise* rose once more, but this time she came down in clear water.

"We're across!" Tud shouted, a note of triumph in his voice.

But now, though the waves were rolling safely along their aft quarter instead of into the boat, she was filling up. The pounding must have opened up a seam.

"Tud! We gotta beach her!" Bailey shouted. "It's comin' in faster'n I can bail!"

"Keep at it, you little chickenshit," Tud replied. "She's not gettin' beached anywheres. We'll go up the creek some and tie her up at one o' them fancy-pants docks at Tanners Neck. Then we can think what to do next."

Bailey knelt on the deck, right knee braced against a rib, left foot jammed against the engine box as he scooped up bucket after bucket of water and pitched it back over the side. *I'm going to lose my toes*, he thought, oddly detached from the reality of it. The chasing waves couldn't catch them now as they skated into Cardiff Creek. Out of the corner of his eye, he saw a stake whip past, so close it nearly jabbed Tud where he stood at the tiller. A wave frothed past the stake, then it stood in a trough of water, a single, strange stillness in the maelstrom, and in that moment Bailey saw a flash of color.

"Tud!" he yelled, pointing. "What's that?"

"Where?"

"There!" Bailey pointed at the stake that was fast retreating into the veil of sleet. "Turn around!"

"No!"

Bailey dropped the bucket, eyes fixed on the stake to keep it in sight. "I saw something," he insisted. "Turn around."

Tud hesitated, wanting to ignore Bailey, but Bailey pointed again, a bird dog with his quarry in sight. Reluctantly, Tud began to turn *Evelyn Louise* around. The waves came spilling over the side again and he doubted the wisdom of his own insistence, but just as the boat's nose came into the wind again, Bailey saw it, a flash of red hovering around the stake.

"There," Bailey shouted, pointing.

"I don't see nothin'," Tud growled, squinting.

"Get closer," Bailey demanded. It could be anything, but something kept prodding him. He grabbed the boat hook and stumbled forward just ahead of Tud on the starboard side. He clutched the coaming with one half-frozen hand, ready to snag whatever it was.

"It ain't nothin'!" Tud insisted.

"Closer!" Bailey screamed, chest pounding, boat hook extended.

Evelyn Louise pitched miserably as Tud pulled alongside the stake.

"We're gonna go down right here!" Tud shouted, as a wave sluiced along the deck and into the cockpit. He swung the tiller over, sending *Evelyn Louise* around again, but in that split second's hesitation, Bailey had picked it up.

sixteen

"I t ain't nothin' but a life jacket!" Tud snarled angrily. "Probably fell offa some yacht. Get that bucket and get this water outta here!"

Bailey clutched it to his chest, unmoving.

"Dammit, Bailey!"

Bailey raised his head, tears streaming down his face and held the red life jacket up.

"What?" Tud stared.

Scrawled in black letters across the life jacket was a name: Hannah Kraft.

"It's Sis's life jacket," Bailey said, "the one I bought her . . ." He didn't finish the sentence. It was the one he had bought her after she had fallen overboard, when he thought for one awful moment that he had lost her.

"What?"

"Sis's life jacket!" Bailey screamed. "It was on *Leah Jean!*"

Tud froze.

"It blew overboard," he said.

Bailey shook his head.

"It was in the cabin."

"It blew overboard," Tud repeated stubbornly.

"Tud!" Bailey yelled.

"Bail, you little sonofabitch."

Tud refused to acknowledge what it might mean. Instead, he stared upriver toward a little collection of private docks.

"We'll tie her up on the leeward side of one of these docks. Keep 'er from gettin' bashed to pieces. I only got a couple lines. It'll have to do. Goddammit, get that water outta here!"

Bailey stared at Tud for one long moment, then flung the life preserver into the cabin, grabbed the bucket, and started to bail again. They rounded Stoney Point and made for the first of three sturdy new piers jutting out of the protected shore, extensions of privilege. Tud headed for its southern side. Bailey dropped the bucket and pulled out three frayed lines. As the boat slid alongside, Bailey looped one over the first piling, then snubbed it up on a stern cleat to keep the boat from being pushed further ashore by the wind. He tied a second line up forward in a meager attempt to spring the boat fore and aft, tied a bowline, then flung the anchor overboard off the stern to keep her from beating herself against the dock.

The entire time Bailey worked, Tud didn't move. He stood as though mesmerized, hand wrapped around the tiller. After securing *Evelyn Louise*, Bailey shut off the engine, then the bilge pump. No point in letting it run, he thought. She can sink here at the dock. We'll worry about her later. Before closing the cabin door, he picked up the red life vest. With one arm through the vest's armhole, he crossed the slick deck.

"Come on, Tud."

Tud remained frozen in place.

"Tud."

Slowly, with obvious effort, Tud turned his head to look Bailey full in the face, but there was no recognition in the eyes.

"Come on," Bailey said again, this time, reaching over and peeling Tud's hand off the tiller. "Come on. We're gonna go up to the house now and call Mom."

He shot a glance toward a large brick home just visible through a fairyland of white. Everything—leafless trees, grass, stone benches, and the BMWs and Volvos parked along the curved driveway—was coated in gauzy layers of ice.

Tud swept a bewildered stare around the boat. Water was already rising over the floorboards, the bucket half floating on its side by the engine box.

"It's all done, Tud," Bailey said. "Come on. Get your foot up. It's time to go."

Wrapping his arm around the strut, Bailey pushed Tud up onto the dock where he stood gaping like a newly hatched chick. Then Bailey climbed up too. He took Tud's arm and guided them haltingly toward shore, aliens venturing abroad in a new and unfamiliar land. When they reached the house, Tud drew back. Behind glazed windows they could see laughing, velvet-clad people moving through opulently decorated rooms, crystal glasses in hand.

"I can't," Tud breathed, stopping beneath an old locust whose branches hissed and clattered in the wind. The ground beneath the tree was littered with downed limbs. Bailey pulled Tud out into a clearing in the driveway.

"Wait right here," Bailey told him.

He set off toward the house, the red life jacket still slung over his arm. At the back door, he hesitated. Inside, he could hear voices and the sounds of children running. An oven door slammed shut, followed by a peel of laugher. Celebration. Human connection. It made Bailey feel more empty. Taking a breath, he balled up his fist and pounded on the door. He heard footsteps, then the door opened and the aroma of roast goose and pumpkin pies enveloped him. A woman dressed in satin covered with an apron, her hair slicked back to reveal ears studded with large diamonds, stared at Bailey as though he had just stepped off a shuttle from Mars.

"My God!" she cried. "Where did you come from?"

"May I use your telephone?" Bailey asked without bothering to answer her question.

"Of course! Come inside! Where did you come from?" the woman asked again, leading him to a portable phone on a counter.

Focusing on the task at hand, like a drunk with limited powers of concentration, Bailey took the phone and dialed home. Emma picked it up on the first ring.

"Mom?"

"Thank God!" her voice broke and he could hear her crying.

"Mom, I need you to come get us," Bailey said, unaware his voice was shaking.

"Did you—?"

"We're down on Tanner's Neck somewhere," he cut in.

He didn't trust himself to answer questions. Questions and answers would feel too much like reality. Right now, he needed to believe it was all a horrible dream. It helped him keep putting one foot in front of the other.

Several expensively dressed children screeched through the kitchen then catapulted through a swinging door into a candlelit dining room.

"Where exactly are you?" Emma asked.

"I . . . I don't know," he said. His seeming calm faltered, and he looked at the woman who had stood by while he talked.

"Do you want me to give someone directions?" she asked,

Bailey nodded, handing the phone over without another word. He leaned back against the wall and closed his eyes, hoping to blot it all out.

"Is that your mother?" the woman asked after putting the phone back into its cradle.

Bailey nodded without opening his eyes.

"I feel as though we should have asked you to just stay and have Thanksgiving here with us," she said, without conviction. "It's awful out. The radio says it's one of the worst ice storms of the century. She probably shouldn't be out on the road tonight."

"She'll be all right," Bailey told her. He longed to be away from this cozy luxury, the assumption of security that mocked the life he led.

"Why don't you take off your wet things and I'll get you something hot to drink."

Bailey opened his eyes, shook his head, and heaved himself off the wall.

"I gotta go back out," he said.

"No, you wait inside. It's dreadful out there," the woman told him.

"Tud . . . ," Bailey began.

"What? Is that your dog?" she asked.

Bailey started toward the door.

"He can come in," the woman said. "We'll put him on the porch. It's no fit night out for man or beast."

She opened the door and saw Tud standing in the driveway, arms at his sides in defeat.

"My God, you can't leave him out there in this. Go get him. I'll give you both a brandy."

Bailey stumbled back outside and across the lawn to Tud.

"Come inside, Tud," Bailey said.

Tud shook his head.

"Come on, Tud," Bailey urged. "It's warm in there."

"No."

"Tud, we're both lookin' at frostbite. Come inside," Bailey insisted.

"No!"

"Mom's comin' for us. You're gonna lose some fingers and toes if you just stand out here like this."

"What does it matter?" Tud asked, miserably. "What does it matter?"

Bailey had no persuasive answer to that, but he grabbed Tud's arm and hauled him toward the back of the house. The door swung open— the woman had been watching them; she stepped back and let Bailey push Tud inside.

"Elise, go get a couple of tumblers and pour some brandy into them," the woman told a pretty teenager who trotted over to a cherry-stained cabinet and pulled out a bottle and a couple of glasses with suspicious ease.

The girl handed a glass to Bailey who turned and offered it to Tud. Dull-eyed, Tud merely gazed at him until Bailey put the glass to Tud's lips and poured some into his mouth. Tud swallowed automatically but made no move to take the glass.

The woman watched, squinting worriedly, but said nothing. They were like wounded animals, afraid, ready to snap, and she dared not come too close. People burst in and out of the kitchen—curious but unwilling to question the incongruity of the two strangers. Family and guests gathered up the pieces of the feast they would soon share, darting surreptitious glances at Tud and Bailey huddled together in a corner. Finally, the woman removed her apron, folded it, and put it across a chair.

"Can I fix you a plate?" she asked.

Bailey shook his head, unable even to muster the "thank you" he knew he owed her. She had put towels down where their foul-weather gear was forming a puddle like a little moat on the floor around them.

"If you change your mind . . . ," she trailed off uncertainly, then escaped through the swinging door to the dining room where her world was intact, unshaken.

Standing in the corner of the kitchen, Bailey looked around at the gleaming surfaces, custom-made cabinetry, a huge six-burner stove and vast refrigerator, a case of champagne that whispered effortless abundance. On the counter lay a silver platter the size of a shield laden with the remains of a half-bushel of raw oysters—the rich appetizer made possible by people like him and Tud . . . and Booty.

So this is what it's like, Bailey thought, looking around. They buy us, bushel by bushel, day by day. Our lives are poured into supplying theirs. They will never know enforced sacrifice, true self-denial. Envy threatened to choke him.

He was dazed, light-headed in the kitchen's steamy heat. After what seemed like hours, children, followed by a few female adults, trooped back into the kitchen with the remains of roast goose and turkey and stuffing, homemade cranberry compote and onion confit. Bailey began to worry that his mother had run off the road. He was on the verge of panic when he heard a knock on the back door. He opened it to find Emma, clad in Orrin's foul-weather jacket, her face nearly hidden in the cavernous hood. Without a word, he grabbed Tud and slipped out, shutting the door behind them.

When Emma saw Tud, she began to cry quietly, her hand held over her mouth. They made their way to the station wagon, Bailey still holding the red life jacket over one arm. Inside the car, Sis crouched in the front seat, eyes wary. Bailey opened the back door, shoved Tud inside, and slammed it. Then he skidded around the back of the car, climbed into the other side, and dropped the life jacket between them on the seat.

"Bailey?" Sis whimpered as her eyes fell on the life preserver.

"Shut up!"

It was the last thing anyone said before they slid into their driveway nearly two hours later.

seventeen

By the time they got home, Tud was limp. Together, Bailey and Emma pulled him from the car, brought him inside, and stripped off his gear in the mudroom, leaving it in a stiff pile on the floor. Beneath the slicker, he was sodden and stank of sweat and alcohol.

"Lay him on the sofa," Emma instructed.

Bailey did as he was told, negotiating the chairs ringed around the kitchen table with a sense of dread—the empty chairs were a reminder of what was missing—of his father, and now Booty, of other times when life seemed whole, safe. Together they stumbled into the living room, where Bailey dropped Tud onto the couch. Emma went upstairs and brought down a thick wool blanket, the same one she and Orrin had tussled over when Orrin, covetous of its thick warmth for early morning runs, had tried unsuccessfully to smuggle it onto *Leah Jean*.

"Cover him up," she instructed. "I'll make coffee."

Sis had already put the pot on and was pulling out mugs by the time Emma came into the kitchen.

"We ought to get him into a tub," she said to Sis. "Except I'm just not sure how much shock he can take to his system."

"What about Bailey?" Sis demanded.

Emma looked at her, really seeing her for the first time in weeks. Always slim, Sis was now nothing but bone and sinew. Dark circles ringed her eyes. Emma knew they were all worn out with grief and work. It was too much. Ignoring her daughter's implied rebuke, Emma went back to the living room where Bailey was still standing over Tud, whose breath sounded like a rasping bellows.

"Bailey, get out of those clothes and get into the shower," she told her son, touching him briefly on the shoulder.

Sis was pouring coffee into two mugs when her mother came back into the kitchen. Reaching under the sink, Emma pulled out a bottle of whiskey and poured a long measure into each mug, then took the tray, went into the living room, and set it on the coffee table. Tud looked like a bloated fish that had washed up on the sofa.

"Sit up, Tud," Emma said gently.

Sis followed Emma back to the living room as her mother laid a hand behind Tud's head where the stringy gray hairs were plastered to his neck and helped him to raise himself to a half-sitting position. Sis made a disgusted face, sure they'd never get his smell out of there.

Emma lifted the mug to Tud's lips and urged him to take a sip. His eyes opened wide at the unexpected heat, but there was still no recognition in them.

They heard footsteps along the upstairs hallway, then a door slammed.

"Take that up to Bailey," Emma told Sis, nodding toward the second whiskey-laced mug.

Sis took the mug off the tray and obediently headed toward the stairs. As she climbed, she could hear Bailey crashing around his room, but there was silence by the time she reached his door. She hesitated, then taking a deep breath, opened it and stepped inside.

"What?" Bailey demanded. He was sitting on the bed, gingerly pulling on a sock.

"Mom sent . . ." Sis held up the mug, then dropped her gaze to Bailey's bare left foot. The last two toes were purple, nearly black. "Bailey!" she breathed, eyes wide.

"What?"

"Your toes!"

He stopped and followed her stare.

"They'll be fine," he insisted, hurriedly grabbing a sock and pulling it over his foot.

"They won't!" Sis cried, horrified. "I've gotta tell Mom."

"You do an' I'll tell her you fell overboard, which is why we bought that damned life jacket in the first place," Bailey retorted.

"She knows," Sis said softly.

"What?"

"She knows about me going overboard," Sis said again. "Booty told her. That's why she agreed to sell him half the boat."

"What? That can't be right," Bailey said, incredulous. "How could he know? Besides he wouldn't have told even if he did. Tud might've, though."

"Uh-uh," Sis said, shaking her head. "It was Booty."

Bailey held his breath for a moment digesting the thought. The betrayal was complete. For a split second, he was almost glad Booty was gone, a just retribution.

Sis watched the anger wash over Bailey's face.

"Bailey . . ."

"Shut up!" he snapped, turning away from her. His whole life had been crumbling away in chunks, and he was powerless to stop it.

Stung, Sis put the mug on Bailey's dresser.

"Mom put whiskey in it," she said.

Though Bailey refused to acknowledge it, the significance of their teetotal mother doling out alcohol to anyone, let alone her underage son, was not lost on either of them. Bailey took it as one more sign of the collapse of their lives. He pulled the sock over his throbbing left foot, then reached for the mug and took a gulp. The whiskey seared his throat. The physical pains were welcome, something to focus on, combat. He could fight that in a way he couldn't fight the anger and terror and hopelessness he had felt ever since he'd pulled Sis's life jacket from the water. That pain was unquenchable. A wound that would never heal. This pain in his body, he knew from experience, would subside.

THE SMELL OF breakfast dragged Bailey from a fitful sleep. He pulled his sock off and was relieved to discover that his toes were bright red. He wouldn't lose them. By the time he came into the kitchen, shuffling like an old man to keep from bending his toes, Emma had eggs and bacon and coffee on the table. She stood at the sink, washing dishes. Deliberately, Bailey sat down in Orrin's place at the table and reached for the platter.

"Tud's gone," Emma said as she poured coffee into a mug and put it by his elbow.

"Good."

"Bailey, he hurts worse than you do," Emma said softly. "Booty's his son."

"Somebody shoulda told Tud that when Booty wanted to take my boat from me," Bailey snapped.

"Maybe."

"No maybe about it. What kinda father don't want to partner up with his son?"

"The kind that wants his son to do better than he did," she replied evenly.

"Tud wasn't like that. He wasn't like Dad. Dad wanted . . . ," Bailey faltered, then returned to what he saw as certain. "Tud just didn't want anyone to do better'n him."

Emma studied him for a moment, his head down like a defensive animal's as he shoveled eggs onto his plate.

"We can't abandon him, Bailey."

"Why not?" Bailey wanted to know. "He abandoned Booty."

"He loves Booty."

"He sure has a lousy way of showin' it."

"Yes, he did . . . ," she agreed slowly, musing on the thousand ways that people love each other, and the thousand ways they hurt each other with that love.

"He's the reason Booty was out there in the first place," Bailey said.

"Tud wasn't the only reason," she reminded him. Her words cut through him, an accusation as well as admonition. "Bailey, we aren't the kinda people that abandon people in trouble."

Bailey glared but couldn't refute her.

"DNR oughta have a helicopter out by now to search," he said finally. "I'll go down and see what's goin' on."

"You're gonna hafta wait on me and Sis. You two have off school, but I want to get to work today—I can use the hours and I don't want you to leave Sis alone."

"Why do I hafta wait on you?"

"Because Tud took Dad's truck. I'll drop you. He's bound to leave it at Hanson's."

"He better have," Bailey muttered, rising and shuffling toward the mudroom.

"Why are you walking like that?"

Bailey ignored her.

"Bailey, why are you walking like that?" Emma said again, catching him by the sleeve.

"It's nothin'," he said, shrugging her off. He was tired of being treated like a child. He was pretty sure his toes would come through intact, but if they didn't, it was his business, not his mother's.

Emma studied him for a moment. A vein in Bailey's temple throbbed and she could see the pulse in his neck, but he stood rigid, every fiber in him leaning away from her.

"Can you drive?" she said finally.

"Yes."

"I'll get Sis up and we'll go."

The sleet had stopped in the night, but every blade of grass, every remaining leaf was encased in glittering ice. Under other circumstances, it would have been beautiful. Now, it was just another obstacle. The roads had been plowed and salted. On his way through, Jake McCall, who drove the state roads salt truck, had stopped and salted the Krafts' driveway too, a gesture of the friendship that he and Orrin had shared since boyhood, a friendship that Orrin's family had, by virtue of the good-ole-boy code, inherited automatically.

Sis sat curled in the back seat, the egg-and-bacon sandwich Emma had foisted on her shoved in her jacket pocket, oozing grease. Bailey revved the motor and eased out of the driveway, navigating the empty roads with a care Sis had never known him to exercise before. She could feel his fear, or maybe it was reluctance.

By the time they crept down Cannon Street into the parking lot, it was nearly ten. The dock lines and running rigging on the few unkempt sailboats in slips were all stiff with ice, but the wind had died down and, except for the wadded gray clouds that stretched overhead like a cotton wool blanket, the day was clear. Orrin's truck was parked next to a green Department of Natural Resources pickup with an empty trailer hitched to it. A knot of men huddled by its grill. It wasn't until he came closer, each step sending hot jabs of pain along his feet, that he saw Tud, head down, eyes on the ground in their midst.

"What's goin' on?" Bailey nudged Rob Boss, who stood like a mute ox at the periphery of the circle.

Rob turned a mournful face to Bailey.

"The helicopter spotted a boat like *Leah Jean* fetched up on Torys Prize."

Nausea nearly overwhelmed Bailey, and he could hear the blood swarming in his ears. Rob's lips moved again, but Bailey couldn't make out what he was trying to say.

164

"What is it?" Emma asked, coming up beside them.

"They found somethin'," was all Bailey could manage.

Iggie waded through the crowd to where they stood.

"You don't hafta go, Bailey," he said without preamble.

"Go?"

"The DNR're goin' downriver in the Whaler to where they saw the boat. You don't hafta go."

"*Leah Jean*'s my boat."

Iggie glanced at Emma, then back to Bailey.

Bailey looked through the thicket of men to Tud. His face was like stone, his eyes fixed on some point in the distance, removed from his immediate surroundings. Several men pressed in on him—protective but silent.

"I'm goin'," Bailey said.

Iggie nodded without comment.

Carefully, making an effort to walk normally, he made his way toward Tud. The two uniformed DNR police had broken off from the clump of watermen and were headed for the Whaler that they had launched and tethered to a piling. Tud followed. He clambered stiffly down into the large boat and claimed the seat just ahead of the console, facing forward. Bailey eased himself into the boat and slumped onto the forward platform, gingerly trying to position his aching feet.

One of the DNR police started the motor while the other stepped aboard and cast off. The helmsman moved the throttle forward, and the boat nosed away from the shore. Once they had cleared the docks, he pushed it up to full speed. The Whaler's bow surged up out of the water, sending spray cascading down each gunwale like handfuls of white diamonds. They whizzed downriver, the hull beating heavy time against the waves.

The shore, encased in ice, was littered with broken tree limbs, a shredded boat tarp, and several life jackets that showed up against the dull background like the bright flags on surveyor's stakes. At Melton Point, a great blue heron, his painted head bent low toward the water, stilt-walked around a beached fifty-five-gallon drum.

As they cleared Rebels Neck, Tud sat up, craning toward Torys Prize. A chill ran down Bailey's back. Until that moment, the trip had felt surreal, dreamlike. But now there was an all-too-real anticipation. The DNR police, who had remained silent for most of the ride, leaned toward one another to exchange a few sentences. The helmsmen inclined his head toward the island. The other squinted, then reached into a bin at his knees to pull out a pair of binoculars and train them on the shore ahead.

"I see something."

The officer's words cut through the motor and the hollow pounding of the boat's fiberglass hull. Bailey followed the officer's line of sight, but without binoculars, all he could see was the crusted shoreline. Tud half rose to peer into the distance, but the boat lurched and his knees gave way, dumping him back onto the seat. They were skimming unimpeded over the expanse of water that yesterday had been virtually impassable, quickly closing the gap between them and the shore of Torys Prize. Squinting, Bailey scanned the low tree line, keeping his focus just above where an object might have appeared. It was a trick for locating unlit buoys in the dark that his father had taught him. "You often see something better when you're not looking directly at it," he had told Bailey. Bailey was beginning to understand that it applied to more than buoys.

At the edge of his vision, he saw something move, swaying with the rhythm of the waves, a little way off the beach. As they drew nearer, he could pinpoint it but could not discern an outline. He glanced back at Tud, who was clinging to the console rail, left hand balled into a fist as though to attack, or maybe ward off whatever was coming. The two DNR officers spoke, but to each other only; their words were lost to Bailey and Tud in the sound of wind and motor.

Bailey hoped it was a dinghy, just another piece of flotsam blown from one of the piers. But when he looked again, he could make out a large wedge of white gently swaying in water. His heart started to pound and his breath came in snatches. As they closed the distance, he knew he was looking at the half-submerged prow of *Leah Jean*.

The officer slowed the Whaler and studied the chart he had pulled from beneath the seat.

"We're gonna come down on it from the bow," the one with the binoculars told Tud and Bailey. "Water's shoal in there."

As they idled in toward shore, Bailey could see her, resting lightly on her port side, on the shallow ledge at the entrance to Church Creek, her bow pointed upriver. Years ago, he and Booty had wandered in the sheltered basin with dip nets in hand, scooping up crabs and dumping them—scrambling and snapping at one another—into a bushel basket that floated in a life ring that Bailey had leashed to his belt. When they had returned home that evening, scooting up the river in a borrowed skiff, they had felt like conquerors, ushered into manhood among those who provide for their families.

The officers maneuvered the boat parallel to *Leah Jean*'s starboard rail, inching their way in toward shore in an attempt to circle her without grounding the Whaler's motor.

As they came around the bow, Bailey thought he saw something floating off her starboard rail, a yellow bubble, like a large balloon.

"Oh God!" Tud wailed, letting go the console and scrambling past Bailey, nearly knocking him overboard.

One of the officers shook his head and the other opened up a box and pulled out rubber gloves. Tud hung over the bow of the Whaler, reaching toward the balloon. Then Bailey realized what it was. He retched and clapped a hand over his mouth. His stomach contorted again and his breakfast came up, spurting through his fingers. He leaned over the side and retched until he was empty.

They had sidled up to the submerged port side, with its grim catch held to the boat by a line. Tud leaned out, reaching toward the yellow foul-weather gear. "Stupid kid!" he screamed. "You could have walked to shore!"

The officers exchanged looks, then the second one came up behind Tud and put a hand on his shoulder. "Let me do this," he said calmly, gripping Tud and firmly pulling him back into the boat.

The helmsman had thrown the engine into neutral and reached out to grip the edge of *Leah Jean*'s canopy, which was canted toward the water like a deflated tent, while his fellow officer kneeled down on the flat forward decking near Bailey. Reaching over the side, the officer grabbed the half-submerged sleeve and pulled. Bailey felt another wave of nausea. He retched again, then forced himself to turn back and look.

A gloveless hand, white, puckered, came out of the water and the officer reached into his pocket and pulled out a knife.

"What are you doing?" Bailey yelled in a panick.

He lunged for the officer, who, larger and stronger, shook him off and turned to look Bailey in the eyes.

"He tied himself to the boat," he explained. "I need to cut the line to get him aboard."

Bailey stopped. Tud was on his knees beside the officer, hands wrapped around the rail, transfixed on the lifeless body of his son. The officer maneuvered the limp body around until he could see the line that Booty had tied around his middle, the line meant to be his lifeline in case he were washed overboard, the line that had trapped enough air in his foul-weather jacket to keep his body afloat for them to find. Leaning out, the officer sliced the cord with one swift motion, still holding Booty's yellow sleeve with his other hand.

The helmsman came forward and reached out for the jacket.

"Go on over to the starboard side, son," the helmsman told Bailey. "We got too much weight over here."

Numbly, Bailey did as he was told. From where he sat on the starboard rail, he could see Tud, frozen in place, his face a caricature of horror. Bent over the side, the officers grunted and pulled. Bailey heard boots hit the deck with a sickening squelch, then saw the helmsman reach into the box and pull out what looked like a long zippered garment bag.

"No!" Tud cried.

"It'd be better if we used the bag," the helmsman said.

"I want to see his face!" Tears were streaming down Tud's cheeks.

Bailey thought he would be sick again as the two men rolled the body over. They waited as Tud crawled from his perch in the bow and stood over Booty's body, steadying himself on the rail.

"Stupid kid," he whispered. "Stupid, stupid kid."

He ran a shaking hand through his hair and stared, his face crumpled in on itself. "You want to come see what you and he done?" he demanded, looking up at Bailey.

"Now, none of that," the helmsman said firmly.

The two officers exchanged glances, then leaned down to work the body into the bag and zip it shut with a revolting finality.

"Sit down," the helmsman told Tud. "We're goin' back in."

Tud obeyed, collapsing on the forward console seat. Not daring to move, Bailey clung to the rail as the two officers took up their positions at the controls, swung the Whaler around, and headed back to Elizabethtown.

eighteen

"**Y**ou're goin' and that's all there is to it," Emma informed Tud, who sprawled on the sofa in his unkempt living room, reeking of liquor and vomit. Grizzled stubble covered his face, and his hair smelled like bilge. "I don't care what shape you're in. You're not gonna miss your son's funeral. Bailey, get him off the sofa and into the shower."

Bailey stared at Tud with revulsion. Tud had stayed drunk since they had come back up the river three days before, departing the boat and its heartbreaking cargo without looking back. It was Emma who had arranged the funeral, called friends, knit up the web of caring that surrounds lives in a small community. She had phoned Tud to be sure he was ready, but when she got no answer, she went to his house. Sis, who had disobeyed her mother's order to stay in the car, stood frozen in the shelter of the kitchen doorway, trying not to touch anything.

"I ain't goin', woman. This whole thing is yours, not mine," Tud snarled, recoiling from Bailey's reluctant grasp. "Booty's dead. He ain't comin' back no matter how many hallelujahs everybody says. What's the point?"

"You need to say goodbye to him."

"I done said all my goodbyes."

"A long time ago," Bailey muttered.

"What's that you say, chickenshit?" Tud turned to glare at Bailey.

"I said you cut Booty loose a long time ago," Bailey barked.

"Why you—" Tud tried to lunge off the couch at Bailey but missed and landed on his knees on the floor.

"Get him up," Emma commanded, her patience ebbing.

"No."

"Bailey, I said get him up."

"Why does it matter if he goes or stays? He never cared about Booty. None of this woulda happened if he'd only taken Booty on as partner when he asked."

The room was electrified with stillness that was broken only by Tud's rasping breath. Slowly, like a sleepwalker who had fallen over an object he was unaware existed, he dragged himself back up on the sofa, where he collapsed into the worn upholstery.

"He wanted to take over from the old man. I couldn't have that," Tud said finally. "He wasn't ready. But I'da let him be my partner one day. I just didn't want him thinkin' he could go out on *Evelyn Louise* without my say-so. I didn't want to lose him."

"Well, you lost him now!"

"Bailey!"

"Yeah, I lost him now," Tud agreed.

"Get him up, Bailey," Emma said again. "Get him cleaned up. He's goin' to say goodbye to his son."

"I ain't set foot in a church since Lottie and me was married," Tud objected as Bailey and Emma yanked him off the sofa and steered him toward the bathroom. It was the first time Bailey had heard him speak her name.

"God's prob'ly been missin' you," Emma observed as she grunted under Tud's weight.

"God don't know I'm alive!" Tud growled.

"He knows you're alive all right," Emma snapped, "or He wouldn'ta given you Booty. That boy spent half his life tryin' to make up for Lottie goin'. Now you're gonna show him a little appreciation for the kind of son he's been to you."

Bailey wished his mother would just stop talking and go, leaving Tud all crushed in, collapsed on the sofa with a half-finished bottle of whiskey. At least that would be some kind of continuity, some familiar territory. But Emma was plowing ahead.

"Sis, make a pot of coffee if you can find something to do it with," Emma called over her shoulder. "For Booty's sake, we're not going to be late."

BY THE TIME they got to the church, the stream of people shuffling in the doors had waned to a trickle. A funeral for the old is laced with wistfulness, a kind of resignation. But a funeral for the young is bitter—for missed possibilities, for shattered hope, for the irrationality of death. "These boys, these boys," one slim middle-aged woman was saying as she mounted the steps with her husband, who dabbed at his face with a handkerchief.

Bailey and Emma came up the walk with Tud between them, his hair slicked down wet from the shower, dressed in an ill-fitting jacket. He walked carefully, putting one foot down and then the next as though worried that any moment the pavement would give way. Sis trailed behind like a reluctant flower girl. As they stepped across the threshold, the organist began to play "Nearer My God to Thee."

"I can't do this," Tud said, stiffening.

"Yes, you can."

Emma tightened her grip and leaned forward, forcing him into the narthex.

"Tud?"

A slim woman with a cloud of dyed blond hair stepped out of the shadowed entryway. Tud stared at her, trying to focus.

"Tud, it's me, Lottie."

Tud reeled, almost taking Bailey with him.

"What the hell're you doin' here?"

"He's my son, too," she said defensively.

"Not so's you'd notice," Tud replied, forgetting that it was the same accusation Bailey had hurled at him not an hour before.

An usher came up behind Lottie and leaned around her to stage whisper to Emma, "Mr. Keller wants to know are you comin' in?"

"Tell him . . ." Emma glanced at Tud and Lottie and hesitated.

"Tell him to go ahead," Tud finished for her, pulling away from Emma and Bailey. He turned and staggered back down the steps.

"Tud!"

Tud stalked off, his knees oddly stiff. Bailey longed to go with him. He dreaded this—the church, monument to a hopeful guess, the music, the mourners who all wanted something from him—tears, explanations, apologies, some evidence of the sick guilt that gnawed ratlike on his gut. But most of all he dreaded the coffin. He imagined Booty inside, face chalky, or worse, artificially tanned by the mortician, a sad approximation of what should have been. He would be sitting right beside Booty, but Booty was unreachable now. They could never make it right between them again.

"Booty would've done it for you," Emma said.

Sis shuddered and stepped closer to Bailey. Her mother, whom she had always seen as gentle, was now hard, relentless.

"Come sit with us, Lottie," Emma urged.

Lottie shook her head.

"I'll just stand at the back," she whispered.

"Come sit with us," Emma said again. "He's your son, too. Bailey, Sis, let's go."

Tears started in Lottie's eyes and she nodded, falling in behind the three Krafts as they made their way up the aisle, past a forest of stares both sympathetic and appraising. The service was mercifully short. But the worst was ahead: bearing the coffin elevated on a mortician's gurney and draped to cover the mechanics of death, out the door and across the frozen ground to the open grave. At the minister's signal, Bailey approached the elaborate box with five other young men, all blocky sons of watermen dressed in tight, rarely used suits. The aisle of the old church was narrow, built for other people from other times, and they had to walk sideways to get down to the door along with the coffin. Once they reached the narthex, they heaved the ornate box off the gurney and carried it with difficulty down the salted steps, while behind them, pew by pew, the mourners followed.

As they approached the open grave, Bailey was overcome with a wave of nausea. Clamping his teeth together, he swallowed hard and darted a glance at the others. Across from him, Ralph Bothley grunted, both hands on the gold-colored handrail, and he could hear Earl and Chambliss Gravely behind him panting with exertion. Each appeared to concentrate only on the task at hand, much as they focused on hauling in seine nets, careful to lose none of their catch. Their single-minded focus calmed Bailey.

They passed rows of granite markers that represented generations of watermen—those who had been fortunate enough to die in their own beds after a long life, as well as those whose bodies were never recovered.

Tud had disappeared. Lottie, Emma, and Sis sat in the five chairs lined up at the open grave. Bailey and the others took the coffin to the elaborate framework erected over the hole and, at the undertaker's professionally modulated instructions, slid it across the rollers and into place.

"I am the Life and the Truth," the minister began.

Bailey didn't hear. He stared off into the woods, not even daring to look at Sis, who had collapsed into Emma's broad side. Then it was done. Friends and acquaintances walked in single file past the coffin, still suspended above the open hole. Some dropped a flower onto its polished surface, others held handkerchiefs to their noses then walked back toward their cars. Some of the older people stood together in groups, comforting themselves with community, saying the same things families and friends of watermen have been saying for hundreds of years.

Bailey didn't want to talk. He wanted to run away, back down to the river, but the river was no longer a comfort. It had betrayed him, too.

"Bailey?"

Sarah touched his shoulder.

"I tried to call about ten times."

"I know. Mom told me."

"Why didn't you call me?"

Bailey shrugged. He couldn't explain why. He wanted her to hold him, to feel her warm skin, rosy with life, against his, to feel—for one, uncomplicated, animal moment—alive. She would have done it. She would have given herself to him, called it compassion and prayed it was more. In those few days, when he was raw with pain and she ached to comfort him, she would have given Bailey anything he wanted. All he had to do was ask, and he knew it, but it would have been just one more thing to feel guilty about.

"I thought we could go out and get a soda and talk. I feel so bad, Bailey. I can imagine how you feel—" She caught her breath when she saw his face.

He turned away to keep from looking at her and saw Lottie, her high heels digging into the brittle earth. He frowned.

"Hi, Sarah," Emma came up behind the two of them with Sis huddled beneath her arm. Sis's pinched face was pale, her eyes bloodshot.

"How'd she know about Booty?" Bailey demanded, still glaring at Lottie's retreating back.

"I called her," said Emma.

"You called her? You knew where she was?" Bailey asked, incredulous.

Emma nodded.

"She'd call from time to time, ask about Booty," she murmured almost to herself. "She'd call, but she wouldn't come back. Not even for

Booty. I don't understand a woman who'd walk out on her family. I could understand her leavin' Tud, but how could she leave that little boy?"

We all abandoned Booty, Bailey thought. Every one of us. Even Mom. She sold him half of *Leah Jean*—not to help Booty but to hinder me.

"I've got food at home," Emma said. "People'll be comin' back. We need to go."

nineteen

₵

I t had only been a week since Booty's funeral, but it seemed like months. A half-dozen times, Bailey had reached for the phone to call Booty, then remembered. Sarah had been dogging him, stubbornly plopping down beside him every day in the school cafeteria, chattering about her classes, the frustrations of geometry, her struggle to balance a part-time clerking job at Hillman's with homework and band practice, and gently, though unsuccessfully, prodding Bailey to talk about Booty. Bailey sat hunched in silence, hardly even glancing at her. Her insistent concern grated on him. It felt like a demand, ownership of some kind. He didn't want to talk about Booty. He wanted to talk to Booty. Barring that, he didn't want to talk at all. Only Sis seemed to understand, silently dropping into the passenger seat in the truck every morning and climbing in again in the afternoon when he pulled up to the curb along with the carpooling mothers. But when he came out of school Friday afternoon, Sis was already sitting in the truck, her coat pulled tightly around her.

"I want to go down to the river," she told Bailey.

Bailey studied her for a moment, hesitating, then started up the engine and swung out of the parking lot headed for town.

When they got to Hanson's, Sis climbed out and marched down the dock, arms folded across her thin chest. When she reached the end, she leaned against a piling and squinted downriver. Bailey walked down the pier behind her, his fists stuffed into his jacket pockets. As he came up behind Sis, she pointed.

"There. That stupid Michael was right. They raised *Leah Jean*."

"What?"

Bailey stared at the lone boat that had just rounded the point and was headed upriver.

"It's *Leah Jean*, all right," Bailey breathed. "But who's . . . ?"

Leah Jean was the only boat still heading in. The other watermen were already tied up and unloading their catch. Iggie, who had seen Sis burst out of the truck followed by Bailey, stopped unloading and came up behind them.

"We took him downriver and raised her the day we buried Booty," he said without preamble. "It was the only thing to do."

"It wasn't the only thing to do!" Bailey turned on him. "*Leah Jean's* mine! Ours! What gives you the—"

"It was the only thing we could do to save him, Bailey," Iggie interrupted. "Bein' a waterman's all he knows"

"He don't even know that!"

"Tud's a decent waterman," Iggie replied mildly.

"He ain't!"

"Let it go, Bailey," Iggie advised. "You got enough to carry already."

Bailey glared at Iggie, who shrugged and turned away, ambling back down the dock to where his nephew was loading the last of the oyster-filled bushel baskets into the back of Iggie's pickup. Bailey turned back to watch *Leah Jean*—deep-loaded to judge by the height of the thick wave she pushed—plow upriver just outside the channel. He and Sis stood there, hardly moving despite the chill wind of the first of December, until they could see Tud's face. He stood, one gnarled hand on the tiller, scanning the dock in preparation for turning into his slip. Seeing the tiller in Tud's hand incensed Bailey. He willed Tud to see him, to read the fury on his face, the silent promise of revenge for the liberty he was taking.

Dull-eyed with exhaustion, Tud slowed *Leah Jean* to make the turn into the slip. He was just reaching for a line when his eyes fell on the two of them. He faltered. For a second, Bailey thought Tud was going to turn around and head back downriver, but he kept *Leah Jean* idling ahead. As he brought her gently into *Evelyn Louise*'s slip, he reached with practiced ease for the lines that hung on twenty-penny nails hammered into the pilings.

Bailey and Sis watched Tud shut down the engine, close up the cabin, and make ready to unload the catch that was layered in bushel baskets in the stern. Without a word to either of the Krafts, he slid the first basket roughly over the deck, scraping the paint, then bent down and heaved it up onto the coaming. He looked up at Bailey, who stood rigid on the dock, eyes slitted with resentment. They froze for a second in silent debate. Then, out of long habit, Bailey reached down and took the basket handles from Tud and swung the bushel of oysters—nice big ones, he noted involuntarily—onto the dock by his feet.

Tud nodded thanks and stopped, arms at his sides.

"Iggie and a couple of the boys helped to raise her," he said. "When we got 'er back, we pumped out the gas and put in new. Except for a little splutter in her engine, she's runnin' fine."

Bailey acknowledged Tud's report with a nod but didn't trust himself to speak. There was a buzz in his ears, and words spilled over each other in his mind—blaming, venom-filled words. He clamped his mouth shut against them.

Sis stood on the dock, staring at Tud. He looked at her—the image of her father, Tud noticed with a start—hoping for some kindness, but all he saw was anger and bitter Kraft pride.

"It was a good day," Tud said to break the silence. He reached down and grabbed for another bushel.

Bailey stared at him, wondering how any day could be a good day with Booty gone, but he slid the first basket farther along the dock, leaving room for a person to pass, and grabbed the rusted wire handles of the second basket that Tud lifted up to him. Together they unloaded *Leah Jean*, Bailey taking each basket loaded to its rim with Tud's catch and lining it up along the dock beside the others. When *Leah Jean*'s ample afterdeck was bare, Tud locked the cabin door and climbed up alongside the baskets.

"Give me the key," Bailey demanded in a low voice, his hand out, waiting.

Tud looked at the empty palm, young, lean, already callused from years of labor, a near duplicate of Booty's. He reached into his pocket, pulled out the key, and put it into Bailey's hand, then turned to heave the first bushel of oysters up onto his hip and trudge down the dock with it.

Bailey jumped aboard. He turned the key in the lock and opened the cabin door. Inside, the sodden chart book, the one Orrin had bought Bailey when he first began teaching him to navigate, the same one Bailey had used to teach Sis in what seemed now like another life, lay open on the empty bunk. The bunk cushions were gone, along with the spare foul-weather gear that Orrin had kept aboard and the flashlight that had hung from a peg on the bulkhead. It feels like a different boat, Bailey thought, trying to figure out why. Sis's boots hit the deck and crossed to the companionway.

"Come help him, Bailey," she said.

Bailey turned and gave her an assessing look. Her anger had given way to pity.

"He can't do it alone," she prodded.

It was on the tip of Bailey's tongue to say, "He's always thought he could!" But he didn't have the strength. There was a difference in Tud, one Bailey couldn't quite put his finger on. Or maybe it's me, he thought. Reaching for the chart book, he closed it and stuffed it under his arm, then stepped out and locked the cabin door again. He followed Sis up onto the dock and handed her the sodden chart book, then picked up the first bushel basket he came to and started off down the dock toward Tud's truck.

Tud saw him but kept his head down. The pair plodded back and forth like figures on a Swiss cuckoo clock until the truck bed was filled with carefully stacked bushel baskets. After Bailey heaved the last one up, Tud shoved the rust-pitted tailgate up into place with a loud, metallic clang. He paused, hands still resting on the tailgate, head bent as though in prayer.

"Bailey, I ain't tryin' to steal *Leah Jean*," he said wearily. "Your mom told me to fish her. Half o' this goes back to you all."

"So what kind o' deal you make with her?"

"No deal," Tud replied. "She just said fish her. I know what I owe your mama. And she knows . . ." He paused and his hand came up, fluttering in the air for a moment, reaching for some way to explain what it meant to him to be out there, on the river that held his life, his memories, and everything he had dared to love. But words failed and the hand dropped back down to the tailgate. "It's what I can do. Iggie an' some of the boys is gonna help me get *Evelyn Louise* up again, but in the meantime . . ."

"What if you can't?" Bailey asked.

"Can't what? Get *Evelyn Louise* up?" Tud shrugged. "I don't know. Cross that bridge when I come to it, I guess."

The wind skittered around the side of the restaurant and scooped into the truck, wafting up the scents of oysters, mud, and river. As though with one mind, he and Tud both breathed deep.

"Booty and Orrin," Tud said looking into Bailey's eyes for the first time.

Bailey nodded in agreement. It was the smell of their lives—the reek of a spring fish kill, the summer stench of muddy shores at low tide, the tinny smell of a summer squall, and the sweet green fragrance of field corn and shore grass mixed with the slightly salty seaweed that worked its way into the trotline. It was the smell of Tud and Orrin's youth together, the years they had spent with their sons, teaching them to follow the water, the years Booty and Bailey had spent mucking around in the shoals, just as Krafts and Warrens and Bosses and Engels and dozens of other Eastern Shore families had done for centuries.

"Dad always called this kind of day a bluebird day," Sis said, watching Tud and Bailey closely.

"So he did, Sissypants," Tud agreed. "So he did. His daddy always called it a bluebird day, too."

They stood there a moment, listening to the rhythmic thwack of halyards beating against aluminum masts.

"I haven't had nothin' to drink since the funeral," Tud said, eyes focused on the middle distance. He held out a quivering hand then shoved it into his pocket. "I don't know. If I'da stopped drinkin' all those years ago . . ." He stopped and shook off his thought.

Sis stared at Tud open-mouthed, astonished at not only his abstinence but at his confession. But Bailey's eyes narrowed distrustfully.

"That day you all buried Booty," Tud went on, "I was gonna just go home and give up." He paused and looked out over the docks to where *Leah Jean* rocked gently in her berth. "Especially after I saw Lottie. You'd think if she could come back for his funeral she could come back for his life. . . . It must've been me. She hated me that much. But it didn't matter. Nothin' mattered. I just figured, what've I got now? Nothin'. But Iggie and a couple of the boys caught me up and took me with 'em downriver to raise *Leah Jean*. I didn't wanna go when I found out what they was plannin'. But . . . I don't know. Somethin' happened. When I saw her comin' out of the water, like she was bein' born again, I don't know. It's like she was tellin' me she wanted to live. She warn't gonna give up. Booty died tryin' to make himself a life all on his own. I didn't know until right then what guts he had. How he was prob'ly so scared but . . ." Tud dropped his head, eyes filled with tears.

"I didn't want him to leave," Tud finished in a whisper. "Everybody leaves me sooner or later—everybody but Orrin. Then when he died . . ."

Bailey's throat tightened. He knew what he should do now—or at least what Emma and probably his father would have pushed him to do—offer to fish the boat with Tud, to be partners. But he didn't want it. He didn't believe in this sudden change of heart. He had known Tud too long.

Sis stood close beside Bailey. He could feel her lean into his side, whether for comfort or as some kind of signal, a prod to conscience maybe, he couldn't be sure. He was vaguely aware of the sounds of the dock—Earl Sideley revving up his engine, trying to figure out what was causing the knocking while it was running in idle, a gust of raucous male laughter as a couple of men shared a joke before stepping into a pickup, the faint whistling of the breeze as it skudded by his ears. A gull careened overhead, screeching in protest at a hawk that had stolen its dinner.

"Bailey, I can't do this anymore," Sis said finally. "At least not like we've been doing."

Bailey looked at her, her small face shadowed and pinched. She was wraithlike, the bones along her neck visible through skin stretched pale. He knew Sis wasn't strong enough—at least not physically—to keep going the way they had been. But he was still trying to calculate how strong he was, if he could do it alone. He heard Tud's swift intake of breath, and stiffened, anticipating a speech about how much sense it would make for the two of them to hook up together. But Tud's next words took him by surprise.

"I ain't tryin' to take *Leah Jean*, Bailey. I swear. I'm just borrowin' her some. I'll take care of her." Tud sighed, then went on quietly. "I first set foot on *Leah Jean* before you was born. I was smaller'n Sis when your Grampa Kraft bought her. Your daddy and I had some good times on her. And some bad, too. Just standin' on her deck takes me back to them days."

He ran a trembling hand over his face, which, Bailey noticed for the first time, was freshly shaved.

"But them times is gone, Bailey."

"I know that," Bailey snapped, then immediately wished he hadn't.

But Tud refused to anger. Or maybe it had been washed out of him.

"No, I mean all them times, Bailey. It's not just your dad and Booty being' gone . . . though God knows . . ." He sighed. "It's all differ'nt. It's

185

all changin'. Orrin didn't want you to leave. God, how he loved you, the son he had waited for so long. And he loved you lovin' the river. But he loved you enough to push you away," Tud said.

"What?"

Bailey didn't want to talk about this, especially not with Tud.

"When Orrin said he wanted you to go to college, I told him he was gettin' uppity, that he figured a waterman's life warn't good enough for his precious son. But he was right. It's what you gotta do."

"Now, wait a minute."

"No," Tud shook his head. "I gotta say this. Orrin was my best friend. Maybe my only real friend. And he ain't here to tell you this. And maybe I ain't the one to do it either—I know what you think of me. But I owe it to him to at least try."

Bailey stopped and waited.

"You got a gift, Bailey."

"My gift is my nose for finding fish," Bailey interrupted.

Tud shook his head.

"Nope. You're good at that, no lie. Real good. But following the water ain't the only way to use it. Your daddy wanted you to have more choices in your life than he ever had in his. He worked himself to death and your mama's workin' herself to pieces so you can have a chance to make a life they never could have. Your gift is your chances in life, Bailey. And you got a chance to do something that some of the rest of us don't have."

Bailey was stunned. He couldn't make the pieces of this puzzle fit together. Tud had always made fun of folks with book learning and no experience, who made laws that made it harder and harder to earn a living following the water. He had looked down his nose at rich people who thought they were better just because they had more things. That same Tud was telling him to leave his roots and become one of them.

"I don't belong in college," Bailey said. "This here's my home."

"You belong as much as anybody, boy," Tud retorted, a rueful smile curling one side of his mouth. "You're smart and you're a Kraft. River royalty. You ain't just some Yahoo outta nowhere."

Bailey smiled in spite of himself.

"Your daddy wanted to go to college," Tud added.

"What?"

"Yeah, he wanted to learn, whadda they call it? Water . . . no, marine biology. But your grampa wouldn't hear of it. Said that Krafts was bred to follow the water. Then . . ." he glanced at Sis, seemed to change his mind and went on. "Then he and your mom got married, and eventually you came along. And that was the end of that. But he knew even when we was kids that the waterman's life was changin' and that we had to change with it. And if he couldn't do it, then he was by-God determined that you was goin' to."

"But . . ." Bailey's mind reeled. "But why didn't he ever tell me that himself?"

Tud shrugged. "Maybe he woulda in time. Maybe not."

"But, Dad didn't even finish high school," Bailey began.

"That was . . ." Tud paused. "That was something else. Stuff happens. But he had plans. They just didn't always work out the way he wanted. Just like the rest of us, Bailey. But he wanted you to try. He talked about you makin' new footprints and not followin' in someone else's—just like your great-great-whatever-his-name did that came over here from England."

Bailey looked at Tud, then swept his eyes over the dock to the river beyond. His river. It wasn't just that he loved it. He was afraid. But Tud's reminder of his many-times-great-grandfather, Isaiah Kraft—the eldest of ten children, who at the age of seventeen had climbed aboard a ship bound for Elizabeth Town, the new town in the New World—was a challenge. Isaiah's blood was Kraft, too, Bailey reminded himself.

"Bailey," Tud said finally. "If it don't work out, you can always come back. The river'll still be here. But maybe you could be the one to help us figure out how to turn it around. Ya think of that? We all gotta keep on eatin'. That ain't gonna change. Maybe you could help figure out somethin' with that fish farmin' stuff. Somethin' better'n those hare-brained schemes those bookworms done come up with so far. We gotta keep it going somehow. That'd be carryin' on the Kraft name."

Bailey saw a small dark missile hit the water, a cormorant diving for a fish. His father had once told him that cormorants weren't native to Maryland, that they had migrated here. Bailey had never been away from home, away from his river. He couldn't imagine being anywhere else. But then again, not long ago, he couldn't have imagined life without his father, or Booty.

"I don't know if I could even get into college."

Tud shrugged.

"Me neither. All I know is, your daddy put a whole lot of wind in your sails an' gave you the tools to chart your course. Now let's see if you can figure out how to use 'em."

ON HIS BACK in bed, Bailey opened his eyes in the dim light of early December. The sky was an unadulterated sheet of gray outside his window. His eighteenth birthday, a milestone birthday he had expected to celebrate with his father. He had even anticipated his gift: Orrin's announcement that he was a full partner in the boat, Bailey's initiation into adulthood.

But with Orrin gone, Bailey assumed his birthday would be uneventful, just another day. Sis and Bailey to school and Emma to work. His mother might remember to bake him a cake—he and Sis could pick up ice cream on the way home from school just in case—but otherwise Bailey looked for nothing to mark the change. A different kind of initiation into adulthood from the one he had hoped for, but an initiation nonetheless. Yet when he came down to breakfast that morning, he found a red leather box at his place at the table.

"Happy birthday, Bailey," Emma greeted him.

"Thanks, Mom."

Bailey opened the box. Inside was a gold watch already running and set to the correct time, its sweep hand meticulously ticking off each second.

"It's the watch Grampa Kraft gave Daddy on his eighteenth birthday."

Bailey looked at his mother, then back at the timepiece, unmarked by use. He took it out and held it across his cupped palm like a freshly-shucked oyster, then turned it over to read the etched inscription: To my son on his eighteenth birthday. Love Pa.

"It looks like it's never been worn," he said, fingering the stiff leather band.

"It hasn't," Emma replied. "Your dad put it away. Just in case."

"In case of what?'

"In case he had a son."

Bailey darted a glance at Sis, but if she felt envious, she gave no sign. Slowly, he laid the watch across his wrist and fumbled with the buckle. But with only one hand, he couldn't make the untried leather bend enough to work one end of the band into the small gold buckle on the other.

"Can I help?" Emma asked.

Bailey hesitated for a second. *Maybe I'm not meant to wear this*, he thought. *Maybe it's meant to be a keepsake, something to pass on from genera-tion to generation. Like the Kraft genes.*

But in that second, he heard a whisper somewhere in his soul.

Use it, Bailey. Use the gifts you're given.

He held up his wrist for Emma to fasten the band.

"Thanks, Mom. It's great."

He looked at the watch, light glinting off the warm gold, expensive, looking out of place beneath his worn shirt cuff. But it felt good. Like it belonged there.

Despite the lack of fanfare over this birthday, something had changed. Bailey knew that as of that day, he was legally able to defy his mother, was free to make his own decisions, set the course of his own life. He could even sell the watch and make a down payment on his own boat if he wanted.

But with that realization came another. His life, while his own to guide, was also tied inextricably to others. The pull and haul of relationship, gift, and obligation. He owed and was owed, whether he wanted it or not. Even Krafts needed help. Every generation since Isaiah Kraft had depended on the one before it for partnership of some kind or another—support, teaching, advice. Bailey began to think that even Isaiah might not have done it completely on his own. There could have been friends or neighbors, people who put out a hand when he needed it most, people whose names hadn't come down through the generations with the family stories.

Each night, Bailey carefully removed the watch and placed it on the stand beside his bed, a silent companion to his dreams. The leather slowly grew more pliant with use. Soon he could fasten the buckle without help.

THE ELEMENTARY school parking lot was nearly empty by the time Bailey sped down the drive to where Sis waited alone, hunched against a northwest wind at the corner of the main entrance. Leaves swirled and eddied past her feet. It was the final day of school before Christmas holiday, and she was the last one to be picked up. Bailey felt a twinge of guilt.

"What took you so long?" she demanded, crawling into the passenger's seat. "I wanted to walk over and find the truck but Mr. Riley wouldn't let me leave. I was gonna call Mom to come get me."

"Sorry. I had a meeting," Bailey apologized. "It took longer than I thought."

Sis climbed into the cab, dragging her backpack onto the floor. Bailey saw the principal, Mr. Riley, lean out the school door and wave, discharging the last of his students before he could begin his own holiday. Sis waved back and reached for the door, but the wind caught it. Without looking back, she put her left hand out to Bailey, who grasped it automatically. While Bailey kept her in the truck, she leaned way out and grabbed at the door handle. Once she had a firm grip, she just held on and he hauled her back into the cab, the door closing with a metallic *chunk*.

Throwing the shift into forward, he put his foot gently on the accelerator and eased the truck away from the entrance while Sis fastened her seat belt. As she pushed the metal buckle into its catch, her eyes fell on the stack of papers, brochures, and catalogues that sat in a disheveled pile at Bailey's hip.

"What's all that?"

"I met with the guidance counselor this afternoon," Bailey replied.

"Yeah?" she asked.

"Yeah," he began cautiously. "Mrs. Wright says they'd take me at the community college, but I might have a shot at Suffolk University. It's right on the water. Bottom of the bay. And she says they have a real good marine biology department. I'm good at biology."

"Huh."

They rode in silence for a few minutes, then Sis reached for the thick Suffolk University catalogue, which sat on the top of the pile.

"This it?"

He glanced at her lap and nodded. In the dimming light, Sis studied the cover, a full-page color photo of well-dressed young men and women whose skin colors ranged from ebony to coffee-tinted cream, laughing together as they crossed a green lawn. In the background, Sis could just make out a sparkling blue wedge of Chesapeake.

"Bailey, are all the kids there black?"

"There's a white kid there, if you look in the background," he said, trying to laugh. But when he saw her face—serious, questioning, worried—he stopped.

"It's a mostly black college. That's why I might be able to get in. Token poor white." He smiled almost apologetically. "That, and my biology teacher offered to give me a recommendation."

"You okay with that?"

"With what? Being white in a black college? Or being the poor kid?"

"Both."

I dunno," Bailey admitted.

Sis thought a minute. Bailey watched her out of the corner of his eye. He wanted her affirmation and her blessing.

"I'd miss you," Sis said quietly.

"I'll miss you too, Sis," Bailey replied, locking eyes with her for a moment, unaware that he had said that as though he were already on his way. "Mrs. Wright says that it's a really good college, and if I got a marine biology degree there, I could go anywhere, do anything."

"But you wouldn't, would you?" she asked. "You'd come back here, right?"

"That's the current plan," Bailey said, knowing now how easily plans could be capsized or rerouted. He wondered what Emma would say about Suffolk. He could no longer predict her; he wondered if he ever really could.

As Bailey turned the corner onto Fish Hatchery Road, Sis huddled down in the seat, her eyes on the darkening sky. Streaks of rose, gold, and purple were ebbing with the last light. They swung into the driveway. Emma's station wagon sat on one side while Tud's truck was pulled up on the grass, leaving what was once Orrin's parking space open for Bailey. He slid the truck in between the other two vehicles and turned off the engine. Instead of getting out immediately, he sat and listened to the silence for a moment. Overhead, pale stars pricked glimmering holes in an indigo sky. Through the window, he could see his mother stirring a pot of oyster stew while Tud sat at the table, a cup of coffee at his elbow. For two Fridays now, Tud had brought back a bushel of oysters—a gift out of his share of the take—and sat in the Krafts' kitchen, shucking them into freezer containers while Emma made supper. An act of contrition as well as community. For a moment, remembering Orrin in the same chair, Bailey felt a little stab of pain but consciously pushed it away. Tud was trying. Bailey wondered what Booty would have said about Suffolk.

He reached into the back seat, slipping the strap of his backpack over his shoulder, then scooped up the catalogues and hugged them to his chest. Sis watched, her eyes on her big brother.

"Bailey, it's all gonna change, isn't it?"

"It already has."

IT WAS A BLUEBIRD day, rare for August, with a clear sky overhead and a breeze barely whisking the tops of the waves into little white peaks. Bailey leaned against the coaming, his hand resting on the helm, ready to nudge *Leah Jean* to port just enough to make it easy for Sis to snag the float at the beginning of one of the trotlines they had laid out in the lee of the shore. She had grown taller and stronger this summer. Her head was now even with his shoulder, and she could hook her thighs beneath the decking to keep from sliding overboard when she leaned out for the float. It wouldn't be too much longer before she'd be big enough to tong, Bailey thought, though he hoped Tud wouldn't let her. At least not for a while yet.

Tud sat on the engine box, cap pulled down to shade his eyes against the lowering sun, as he spliced two frayed deck lines together. Bailey and Tud had been working *Leah Jean* together full time since Bailey had graduated in May. It was a partnership of necessity, but the weeks of working shoulder to shoulder had rubbed it into a partnership of a different kind. The routines—handing off the dip net and boat hook, gauging the size of the crabs, speculating on the harvest, carting their catch up the dock—had worn down the splinters between them, smoothed the rough places.

It had also helped that whenever Bailey stepped aboard, Tud automatically relinquished the helm. Bailey recognized the respect in that gesture and offered respect in return, listening, consulting, asking not ordering. They were sharing *Leah Jean*, and both knew it. She was the last tangible link in the chain that anchored them to their joined past, to Orrin and Booty, to the generations of Krafts and Warrens who had come before them, whose memories were written in every ripple and eddy, every creek and grass-thatched piece of shore. By the time Sis climbed aboard at the end of June, Bailey and Tud had relaxed into a kind of hopeful trust—not friendship exactly, but something very like it.

The afternoon sun thrust a fat wedge of warmth beneath the canopy, bathing Tud in light and splashing his shadow up against the bulkhead. They were slowly shuttling back and forth among the lines they had set on the broad ledge along the northeast curve at the river's mouth. As he headed almost languidly for the next float, Bailey sucked in a deep breath, tasting beached seaweed drying at the high-tide line on shore, the creosote on the spar buoy that marked the wide shoal, and the salt of the river. He could feel the boat beneath his feet as though it were a second skin, sense the tide hesitating, just at the end of slack water and about to turn, by the way *Leah Jean* rocked between the little waves. He registered all these things with a kind of unconscious pleasure. But at the back of his mind, he was counting down the time until he left for Suffolk University. Only ten more days.

"Let's run one more line before we go in," Bailey said, slowly swinging *Leah Jean* northeast toward a red-topped float.

"Okay by me," answered Tud. "I'm just along for the ride. Keep an eye on the time, though. We don't want the DNR to catch us going over the deadline."

Bailey saw Tud finish the splice, then lay the line on the engine box and roll it back and forth with the flat of his hand, working the lumps out of the newly woven twists of nylon until they realigned with the others.

"You taught me how to splice," Bailey said, abruptly remembering with unexpected clarity the Tud of his childhood, the Tud before the drinking and the anger took over.

Tud looked up and smiled, a genuine smile that gently crinkled eyes no longer bloodshot from too many alcohol-filled nights.

"Yup. You and Booty was just spat then. Took two of you to roll the long splice smooth. Neither one of you had enough weight on you to flatten it on your own."

"I remember," Bailey said quietly.

Bailey waited until Sis brought the trotline up over the roller, then set a course for the float that bobbed in the distance at its other end. He had stopped worrying about how Tud would keep up the boat in his absence. *Leah Jean* now held both past and future—for all of them.

Bailey watched Sis shove a doubler back into the water then wait while two empty pieces of bait thrupped over the roller. A third piece came up with a crab clinging. In one graceful, unbroken swoop, she snatched the crab off the bait and dropped it into the basket. Her every movement, choreographed by her genes, fed the task at hand. Tud studied her a moment, then caught Bailey's eye.

"She's good," he said, nodding approval.

Sis straightened a little at Tud's words but remained focused on the line.

"Yeah," Bailey agreed. "Even if she is still small fry."

"I'm not so small any more," Sis informed Bailey, not bothering to turn around.

"No. You're not." Bailey grinned at her profile. "You could smash Stewie Bevins on your own now."

Sis laughed. No one at school made fun of her anymore. The faint whiff of the river and its harvest that periodically followed her into school had gradually become a mark of respect. The boys especially had grown envious of a job that stamped her as capable beyond her years. She scooped the last crab on that line aboard, then slid the end of it back off the roller with the end of the dip net's hoop.

Tud squinted at the angle of the sun, then looked at Bailey.

"Yeah, it's time," Bailey agreed at the unspoken urging. "Iggy's headin' in. That's always a sure sign. Let's pull 'em."

195

Bailey slowed the boat and threw it briefly into reverse, stopping so Sis could haul the float. In the past few weeks she had managed to pull one or two cinder block weights aboard without touching anything, but she still struggled with their heft and bulk, barely missing taking chunks out of the wooden coaming. So she waited for Bailey or Tud to pull it out of the water for her—the boat was more important than her pride.

"You scared, Bailey?" she asked without preamble, handing the boat hook backward to Tud, who took it and put it beside him on the engine box as she started feeding the line down into the basket at her feet.

"Some," Bailey admitted, knowing her thoughts, like his, were on the coming separation from everything and everyone he had known all his life—home, family, friends, and Sarah.

Bailey was leaving, yet Sarah, whose mother had had visions of an Ivy League education for her only child, was staying. She was going to Adams College, a way to remain close to home and—Bailey knew—to him. Her announcement had stirred a caldron of conflicting emotions in him—guilt, pleasure, relief, sorrow. He could feel the unstated pressure to stay, to build a life with her. Part of him wanted that. He knew he'd miss her warm, and warming, presence, longed more and more for them to belong to each other fully, completely. But, with a window opening onto new possibilities in his life, he discovered he wanted to go too, at least for a while.

Sarah fought back tears the day he had told her he was going away to Suffolk University. But she had thrown back her shoulders, stuck out her chin, and wished him luck.

"Just don't forget where home really is," she had finished, forcing a smile.

"My heart's here, Sarah," Bailey had assured her.

"From the first time I set eyes on you, Bailey Kraft, I knew . . ." She had been unable to finish the sentence.

"If it's the right thing, it'll be there when you're both finished college," Emma had said. Bailey hoped that was true.

"Yeah, I'm kinda scared," Bailey repeated, seeing in his mind a flash of Sarah's blue eyes and blond hair and then an image of the campus of Suffolk with its knots of enthusiastic, chattering students, talking, laughing. "But you know, I'm kind of excited too."

"Really?"

Bailey nodded. Once he had gotten the letter of admission—something he had not dared to expect—he and Emma had driven down to see the university, a small, green, tree-sheltered campus planted on an unobtrusive corner of land along the Virginia shore. The campus was peaceful, even welcoming, but Bailey had felt like an interpoler as he walked beside the straight-backed young tour guide with skin the color of toasted hazelnuts. Except for her skin, the young woman looked much like the children of the wealthy in Mercy County, expensively dressed and sure of themselves. It was a different world from the one Bailey had known, a world he had only seen from the outside. And at Suffolk he had felt doubly outside, one of the few white faces in a sea of color. He had wondered whether they would shut him out, close ranks against him even though those who held the keys had let him in.

As he and Emma had followed the guide along the narrow roads that threaded the campus, they passed curious students who tried not to stare at the unaccustomed white faces. A few students, laden with books and carrying on animated conversations, had smiled as they passed. Yet he'd grown increasingly worried, wondering if he could ever fit—let alone succeed—in a place that seemed so different from everything he had known. Fear had risen thick in his throat and with it the urge to flee.

But when they had reached the cemetery and its Freedom Tree, a massive live oak where the founders of the university had first read aloud the Emancipation Proclamation, the same spot on which they had conceived a university for the newly freed slaves, Bailey was suddenly at home. Beneath that tree, surrounded by the graves of those who had gone before, he had recognized in the university's modest brick build-ings, in the statue honoring the fallen who had fought for freedom, and in his guide's careful, dignified manner, a kinship born of pride. Pride in heritage, in community, in the determination to choose a calling, a purpose, a way of life—and the obstacles that must be overcome for it—that stood at the university's core. At that moment, the fear had begun to recede.

As Bailey slowed *Leah Jean*, Sis began to reach out for the float.

"Wait a minute till I get closer," Bailey said, touching the throttle once into forward then back into neutral.

Sis nodded and straightened, eye on the float. The sun glowed gold against their bodies, highlighting Sis's slim, tanned arms and glinting through the bristles of a beard just beginning along Bailey's chin. His shoulders had broadened, stretching the skin across well-defined mus-cles and tendons, and there were wisps of sun-bleached hair along his breastbone.

"Once they get you aboard them boats down there they ain't gonna let you off," Tud remarked conversationally.

"You think?" Bailey smiled, guiding the boat as Sis worked. "Why's that?"

"You got it, boy. That Kraft nose. Like your daddy. And your granddaddy. Once they figure out that they got their very own fish finder aboard, they'll sell whatever million-dollar gizmos they got and just put you up on the bow," he replied, chuckling.

Bailey snorted, but he was grateful for the words. After Sis retrieved the float, she stepped back and handed Bailey the line so he could bring the second cinder block aboard. He laid the block down gently on deck beside the first, then stepped back to the helm. Cranking up the engine, he swung *Leah Jean* toward the last trotline as Sis heaved the bait bas-ket she had just finished filling over toward the companionway and reached for the next basket without standing up.

"You reminded me then of your granddaddy, Sissypants," Tud observed. "He used to use that same twist of his body when he was shovin' things around. He warn't that much biggern' you. Funny how it goes . . ."

After the last trotline was aboard, Bailey let the boat idle a few minutes, feeling the wind against his face. The sun, a vast orange globe that hung over the skeletal arch of the Bay Bridge, was suspended, halted in the sky as though this day—and their lives together on the river—were endless.

Bailey squinted into the distance at the new condominiums lined up like square-edged teeth along the south shore where the river opened wide toward the bay. An uneven string of white-hulled powerboats was emerging from the marinas, fat beads scattering across blue water. As each cleared the last channel buoy, its fiberglass nose jutted up into the air, pushed by the full thrust of a high-powered engine. "Tupperware warriors," Orrin had called them, "trying to claim the river instead of share it." They far outnumbered the watermen and had for years now. Maybe the river already belonged to them.

Everything moves, changes, Bailey thought. *Nothing stays still. We're all moving with—or against—the tide. The key*, he decided, *is to figure out what direction you're headed.*

"Okay. I guess that's it," he said, as Sis flopped down on the engine box beside Tud.

Bailey swung *Leah Jean*'s bow around, stopping by instinct on a direct line to the buoy at the bottom of Torys Prize, still indiscernible in the distance. Leaning his shoulder against the strut, he drew a deep breath and set a course for home.

acknowledgments

Many thanks to Eric Cornelius, first reader, whose father first told him not to be a waterman, for his encouragement, and to Ashley Gordon for her sensitive editing.

And dedicated to all those who, despite hardship and discouragement, still follow the water.

editor's note

Course of the Waterman is the winner of the 2003 Fred Bonnie Memorial Award for Best First Novel from River City Publishing.

Fred Bonnie was a great friend to the literary community at large, and particularly to the South, the place he called home for many years. He was a gifted author and writing teacher, and he was considered a master of the short story. He was generous with his time and his talent, always ready to help a budding writer.

We at River City Publishing were fortunate enough to publish one of Fred's short story collections, *Food Fights*, and his only novel, *Thanh Ho Delivers*. It is the story of a Vietnamese girl's escape from her homeland after the fall of Saigon and her struggle to make a new life in America. Sadly, Fred died suddenly at age fifty-four while returning home from a book-signing event for *Thanh Ho*. In memory of Fred, the author and the teacher, River City Publishing established this award for best first novel. Just as Fred did, the contest provides opportunities for new writers honing their craft. We hope Fred would be proud.